NATIONS OF THE WORLD

ARGENTINA

Anita Dalal

RAINTREE STECK-VAUGHN PUBLISHERS

A Harcourt Company

Austin New York
www.steck-vaughn.com

Steck-Vaughn Company

First published 2001 by Raintree Steck-Vaughn Publishers,
an imprint of Steck-Vaughn Company.

Library of Congress Cataloging-in-Publication Data

Dalal, Anita
Argentina/ Anita Dalal
p. cm -- (Nations of the World).
Includes bibliographical references (p. -) and index.
Summary: Examines the land, people, and history of Agentina and discusses its current state of affairs and place in the world.
ISBN 0-7398-1279-3
1. Argentina--Juvenile literature. [1. Argentina] I. Title.
II. Nations of the World (Austin, Tex.)

F2808.2 .D35 2000
982--dc21

00–027150
CIP

Printed and bound in the United States
1 2 3 4 5 6 7 8 9 0 BNG 05 04 03 02 01 00

Brown Partworks Limited
Project Editor: Robert Anderson
Designer: Joan Curtis
Cartographers: Joan Curtis and William Le Bihan
Picture Researcher: Brenda Clynch
Editorial Assistant: Roland Ellis
Indexer: Kay Ollerenshaw

Raintree Steck-Vaughn
Publishing Director: Walter Kossmann
Art Director: Max Brinkmann

Front cover: Plaza de Mayo and Casa Rosada, Buenos Aires (background); gaucho on horseback (center); condor (top left)
Title page: cattle are herded into pens so that they can be examined and marked.

The acknowledgments on p. 128 form part of this copyright page.

Contents

Foreword

Since ancient times, people have gathered together in communities where they could share and trade resources and strive to build a safe and happy environment. Gradually, as populations grew and societies became more complex, communities expanded to become nations—groups of people who felt sufficiently bound by a common heritage to work together for a shared future.

Land has usually played an important role in defining a nation. People have a natural affection for the landscape in which they grew up. They are proud of its natural beauties—the mountains, rivers, and forests—and of the towns and cities that flourish there. People are proud, too, of their nation's history—the shared struggles and achievements that have shaped the way they live today.

Religion, culture, race, and lifestyle, too, have sometimes played a role in fostering a nation's identity. Often, though, a nation includes people of different races, beliefs, and customs. Many may have come from distant countries.

Nations have rarely been fixed, unchanging things, either territorially or racially. Throughout history, borders have changed, often under the pressure of war, and people have migrated across the globe in search of a new life or because they are fleeing from oppression or disaster. The world's nations are still changing today: Some nations are breaking up and new nations are forming.

Argentina—the eighth largest country in the world—lies at the southern tip of South America. Its population is largely made up of the descendants of the European settlers who have come to the country since the 16th century. Unlike other Latin American nations, the native, or Indian, populations have played little role in shaping Argentina's national identity. The Argentine people have often felt a divided loyalty between their European past and their Latin American present. Within Argentina itself this conflict has been played out between the cosmopolitan capital Buenos Aires and the independent-minded provinces.

Introduction

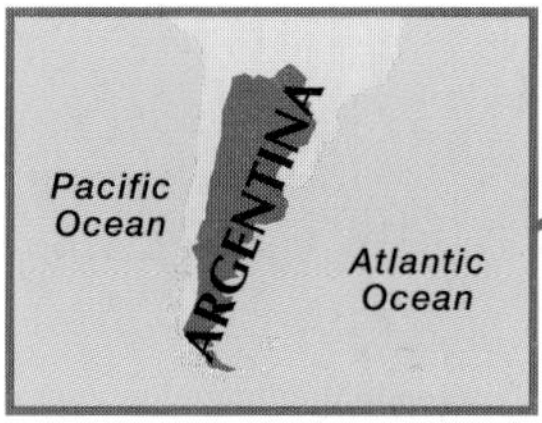

Pacific Ocean
ARGENTINA
Atlantic Ocean

Most people know three things about Argentina: Its people eat beef, love soccer, and dance the tango! While it is true that beef, soccer, and the tango are major parts of Argentine life, there is much more to the country.

Argentina lies in the Southern Hemisphere. Its land area is 1,072,156 square miles (2,776,884 sq. km), making it the second-largest country in South America after Brazil. Argentina is shaped like an ice-cream cone. The widest part of the country is in the north; from here, it gradually tapers to a narrow point in the south.

Argentina shares its northern borders with Bolivia and Paraguay and its eastern borders with Brazil and Uruguay. The soaring Andes Mountains separate Argentina from its western neighbor, Chile. To the east and the south lies the stormy Atlantic Ocean.

The Argentine landscape is very varied. There are lofty mountains and freezing glaciers; vast, flat plains known as *pampas* and tropical rain forests. There are hundreds of deep-blue lakes, and mighty rivers flow from deep within the country down to the Atlantic.

The Argentine people are less diverse than their landscape. Most of the present population is descended from European immigrants, many of whom came from Spain and Italy. Because of the great European influence on Argentina, the capital city, Buenos Aires, is sometimes known as the "Paris of the South."

A familiar sight on the Pampas is the Argentine cowboy, or gaucho. With his fierce independence and restless spirit, the gaucho is a symbol of Argentina.

FACT FILE

- Argentina is the eighth-largest country in the world, only slightly smaller than India. In South America, only neighboring Brazil is larger.
- The name "Argentina" comes from the Latin word *argentum*, which means "silver." The country got its name because of the rich deposits of silver that the Spanish conquerors found in the Andes. However, no silver was ever discovered in Argentina.
- The national flower of Argentina is a tropical tree called the ceibo. In spring, which in Argentina lasts from September to December, it has deep-scarlet flowers.

Argentine bank bills show the heroes of the country's struggle for independence—Manuel Belgrano and José de San Martín.

Argentina is a striking mixture of the old and new. The capital, Buenos Aires, has much in common with modern North American and European cities, Life in the countryside, however, is much more like that of Argentina's other South American neighbors, such as Uruguay or Brazil.

NAME, MONEY, AND FLAG

Since 1860, Argentina's official name has been the Argentine Republic. In Spanish, this is *La República Argentina*, although Argentines call their country simply "*la Argentina.*" The British sometimes call the country "the Argentine," but North Americans generally refer to it as Argentina.

Argentina's currency is the nuevo peso ("new peso"). There are bills of 1, 2, 5, 10, 20, 50, and 100 pesos, and each peso is made up of 100 centavos ("cents"). Almost everywhere in Argentina, visitors can pay with U.S. dollars, so it is not always necessary to exchange dollars for pesos.

The Argentine flag features three broad horizontal bands. The middle band is white with a sun on it, and the two outer bands are sky-blue color. Many people assume that the blue color is a symbol of the immense skies seen in the flat pampas.

In fact, the flag's colors date back to the early days of Argentina's fight for independence. In 1812, General Manuel Belgrano (*see* pp. 59–61) needed an emblem to rally his troops. He adopted the blue and white colors of the feathers of a group of Argentine patriots known as the *patricios*. The radiant sun with a face was added later, and no one is quite sure to what it refers.

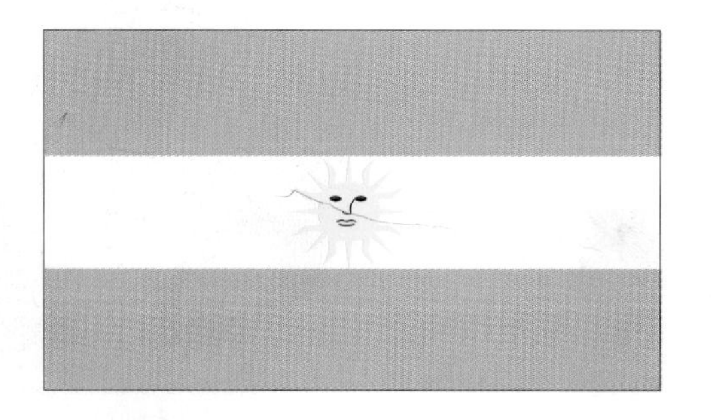

The Argentine flag was adopted in the 19th century. Usually the sun appears only on the flag used by the military. For other purposes, the version without the sun is used.

POPULATION DENSITY

Argentina's population lives mainly in the northeast of the country, where the land is flat and fertile. The most sparsely populated areas are the mountainous lands to the west, the remote region of Patagonia in the far south, and the rain forests of the north.

BUENOS AIRES

PERSONS

Per sq. mi	Per sq. km
13	5
52	20
260	100

POPULATION

In 1998, the population of Argentina stood at almost 35 million. This gives the country the third-largest population in South America after Brazil and Colombia. Some 85 percent of the Argentine population is descended from European settlers.

While most Argentines are of Spanish or Italian descent, the families of others came from Germany, Switzerland, the former Yugoslavia, and Ukraine. Some Argentines are of Middle Eastern descent. The native Indian population of Mapuches, Collas, Tobas, Matacos, and Chiriguanos today amounts to no more than 1 percent of the total. The remaining 14 percent of the population is *mestizo*—that is, people of mixed Indian and European descent.

In the 19th and 20th centuries, Argentina's population grew rapidly as thousands of immigrants arrived from Europe. In recent years, the rate of growth has slowed.

Argentina's population is growing very slowly, at the rate of about 1.4 percent a year. Because Argentina is such a big country in area and has only a small population, the average population density is just 33 people per square mile (13 per sq. km). The vast majority of the population live in the cities of the north. In Patagonia, the remote region that makes up the south of the country, the population is very small and is spread over a wide area.

ARGENTINA'S POPULATION

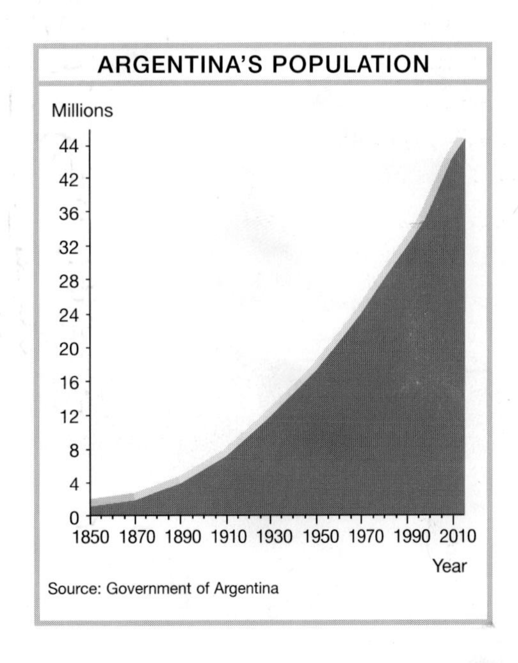

Source: Government of Argentina

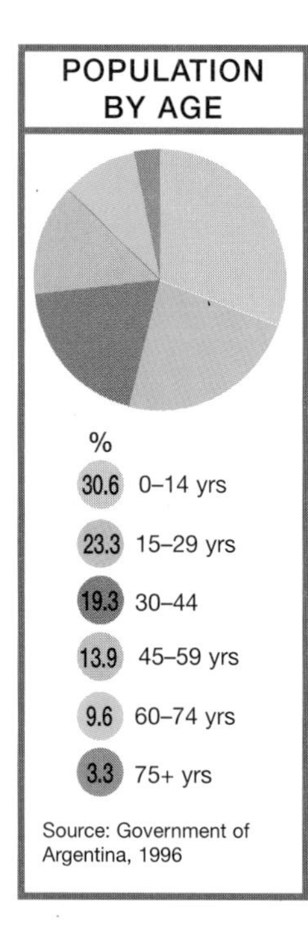

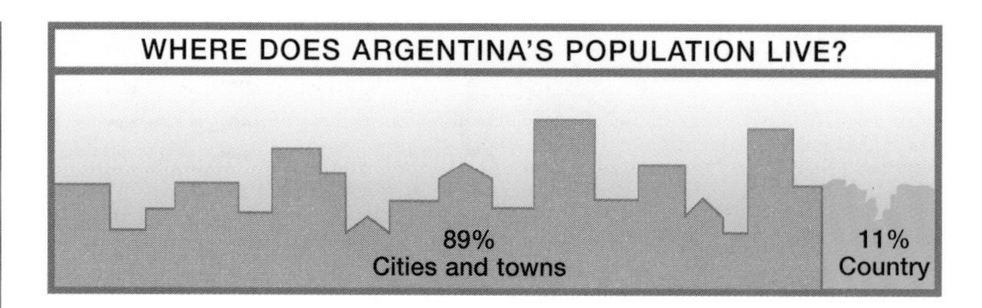

LANGUAGE AND RELIGION

The official language of Argentina is Spanish. Like much of South America, Argentina was settled by Spanish conquerors in the 16th and 17th centuries. Over the intervening centuries, European and American Spanish have developed many differences in pronunciation and vocabulary. There are differences, too, between the Spanish spoken in the various Latin American countries.

The Indian communities of the north and east of the country speak their own languages. These include Guaraní, Quéchua, Mataco, and Aymará. Usually, however, Indians are bilingual; that is, they are able to speak Spanish as well their own language. In Patagonia, a few

Pronouncing Argentine Spanish

Pronouncing Spanish words and names is not difficult. Most letters are pronounced just as they are in English. There are a few exceptions, however:

c	pronounced like *s* when before "e" or "i"; otherwise pronounced like *k*
d	pronounced like *th* in "feather"
g	pronounced like *h* before "e" or "i"; otherwise like *g* in "go"
gu	pronounced like *g* in "go"
h	not pronounced
j	pronounced like a rough *h*
ll	usually like *z in* "azure"
ñ	pronounced like *ny* in "canyon"
qu	pronounced like *k*
r	is rolled
y	like *z* in "azure"
z	is like *s*

Usually in Spanish, words are stressed on the last syllable if it ends with a vowel, "n," or "s." Otherwise it is stressed on the second or third from last. Try pronouncing some of the words you will find in this book: Argentina (arr-hen-TEEN-a), Córdoba (COR-tho-va), Mendoza (men-DOS-a), Tierra del Fuego, (tee-AIR-ra dell FWAY-go).

The National Anthem

The lyrics of the Argentine national anthem were composed in 1813 by the poet and patriot Vicente López y Planes (1784–1856). He wrote them to celebrate the independence of the capital, Buenos Aires, from Spain in 1810. In 1827, López y Planes went on to stand in as a temporary president for Argentina.

Mortals! Hear the sacred cry;
Freedom! Freedom! Freedom!
Hear the noise of broken chains.
See noble Equality enthroned.
The United Provinces of the South
Have now displayed their worthy throne.
And the free peoples of the world reply:
We salute the great people of Argentina!

May the laurels be eternal
That we know how to win.
Let us live crowned with glory,
Or swear to die gloriously.

people speak Welsh. They are the descendants of a group of Welsh immigrants who settled there in 1865. Today, though, Welsh is a dying language in Argentina.

More than 90 percent of the Argentine population is Roman Catholic, although many people do not attend church. Many of the country's most beautiful buildings are connected with Catholicism. These include the Jesuit missions of Mesopotamia in the far north and the beautiful cathedral of Córdoba. There is also a small number of Protestants. Many other faiths are practiced in Argentina, including Judaism, Islam, and the Greek and Russian Orthodox faiths. This religious diversity reflects the different immigrant groups that have come to Argentina over the years.

Respect for the dead is an important part of Argentine culture. National heroes are remembered on the day that they died, rather than on their birthday. Pilgrims to the Recoleta and Chacarita cemeteries of Buenos Aires pay tribute to figures such as Eva and Juan Perón by placing their hands on the tombs.

The charts below show how Argentina's population breaks down in terms of religion and ethnicity.

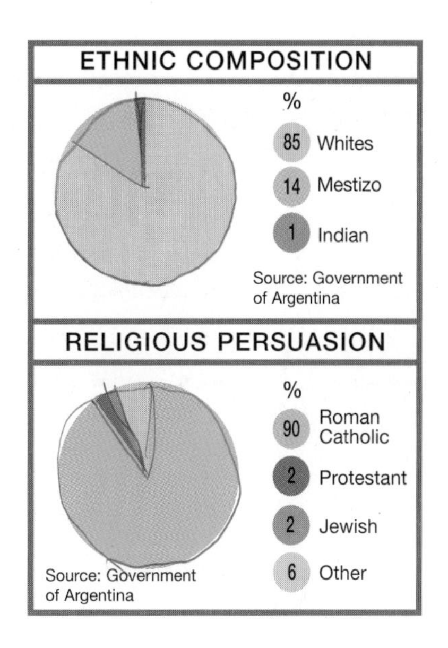

Land and Cities

"The horizon is that of the ocean; an upturned clod attracts attention; a hut looks like a house; a tree looms up like a hill."

U.S. scientist W.J. Holland describing a journey across the Pampas in 1912

Argentina covers an area of almost 1.1 million square miles (2.8 million sq. km) at the tip of the South American continent. The Argentines claim to possess an even larger area. They include as part of their country a number of islands in the South Atlantic that include the Falkland Islands, which they call the Malvinas, as well as a large segment of Antarctica, known as the *Antártida Argentina* ("Antarctic Argentina").

The Falklands/Malvinas and their dependencies are a British colony. In accordance with a recommendation of the United Nations (UN), the islands are often referred to both by their English and Spanish names. By international agreement, Antarctica belongs to no country.

Argentina is dominated by its sprawling, bustling capital, Buenos Aires, where more than a third of the country's population lives. Nevertheless, Argentina's provinces play an important role in the nation's life. Provincial capitals, such as Córdoba and Salta, have their own special character, and their inhabitants have a large measure of political independence from the capital.

Beyond the cities and towns is a vast, beautiful landscape of plains, steppes, grasslands, forests, and mountains, as well as a spectacular coastline of coves, lagoons, and sandy beaches. In these diverse natural environments live a huge variety of animals, birds, and plants, many of which can be found only in Argentina.

Rolling fields of crops and vast blue skies form the characteristic landscape of the Pampas region of Argentina.

FACT FILE

- Under Argentine law, maps of Argentina must show the Falklands/Malvinas and the Antarctic claim as part of the Argentine Republic.
- From its northern border with Bolivia to its southern tip on the island of Tierra del Fuego, Argentina is about 2,170 miles (3,490 km) long—about the same distance as between the southern shores of Hudson Bay in Canada and Havana in Cuba.
- The longest river entirely within Argentina is the Salado. The Salado flows 1,100 miles (1,170 km) from the Andes to the Paraná River at Santa Fe.

During the last Ice Age, the movement of glaciers created hundreds of lakes in the Patagonian highlands bordering the Andes Mountains.

TERRAIN

Geographers generally divide Argentina into four broad terrains: the Andes mountain range; the northeastern lowlands, including Mesopotamia and the Chaco; the Pampas in the middle of the country; and windswept, lonely Patagonia in the south. Each terrain has its own special climate and wildlife.

Mountains and Glaciers

The Andes form the longest unbroken range of mountains in the world. They stretch from the Caribbean coast of Colombia in the north to Cape Horn in the south—a distance of more than 4,500 miles (7,250 km). The mountains run the entire length of Argentina, from its border with Bolivia in the north to the Atlantic Ocean.

The Americas' highest mountain, Aconcagua, lies in the Argentine section of the Andes. Its peak rises to 22,843 feet (6,960 m).

The southern end of the range is lower than the northern. In places, spectacular glaciers (*see* p. 17) stretch across the peaks and reach deep into the valleys on either side. Farther north, in the Andean Lake

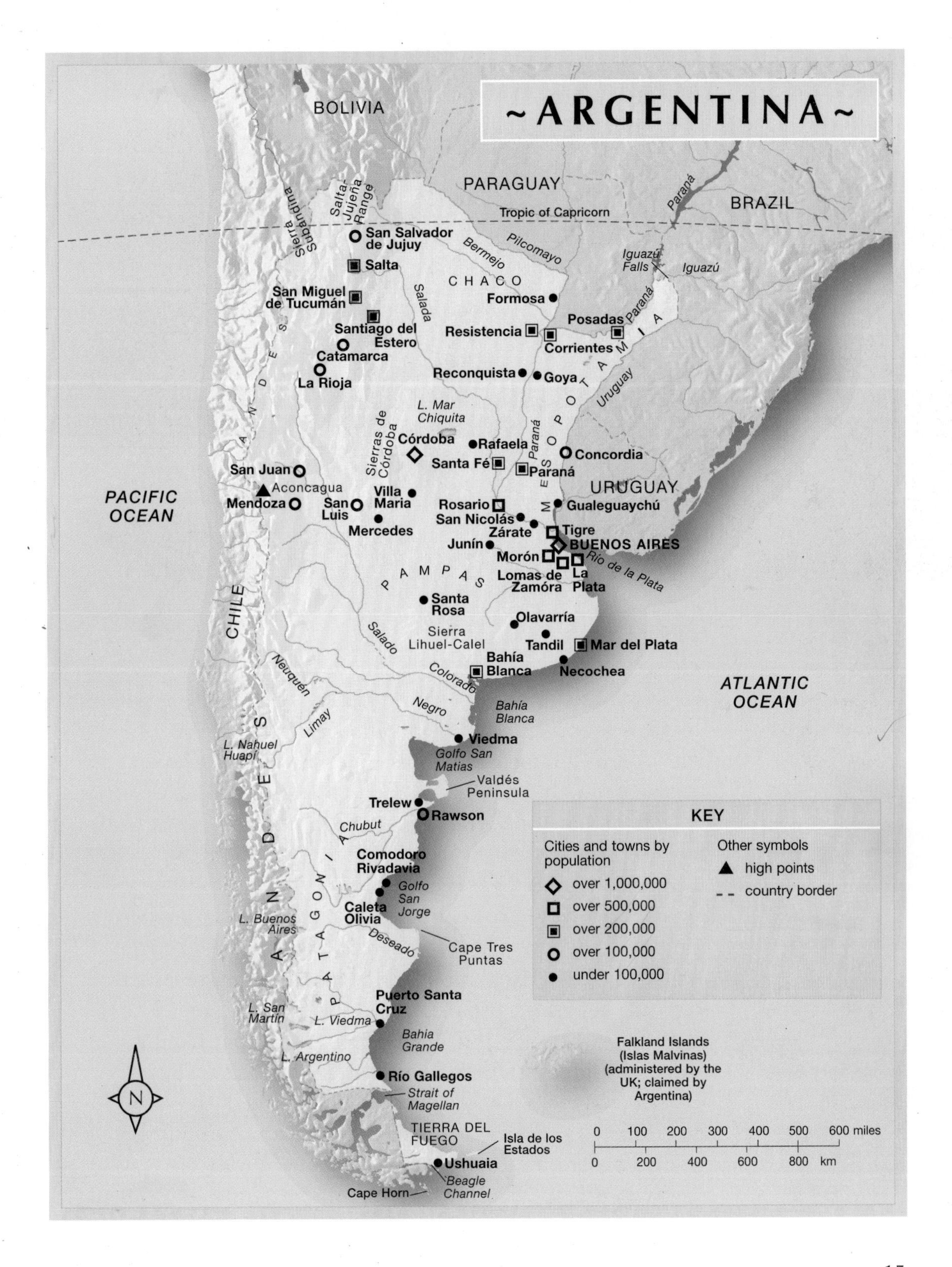
~ARGENTINA~
BOLIVIA
PARAGUAY
BRAZIL
URUGUAY
CHILE
PACIFIC OCEAN
ATLANTIC OCEAN
Tropic of Capricorn
Sierra Subandina
Salta-Jujeña Range
San Salvador de Jujuy
Salta
San Miguel de Tucumán
Santiago del Estero
Catamarca
La Rioja
Bermejo
Pilcomayo
Salada
CHACO
Formosa
Iguazú Falls
Iguazú
Paraná
Posadas
Resistencia
Corrientes
MESOPOTAMIA
Reconquista
Goya
Uruguay
L. Mar Chiquita
Sierras de Córdoba
Córdoba
Rafaela
Santa Fé
Paraná
Concordia
San Juan
Aconcagua
Mendoza
San Luis
Villa Maria
Mercedes
Rosario
San Nicolás
Gualeguaychú
Zárate
Tigre
BUENOS AIRES
Junín
Morón
Lomas de Zamóra
La Plata
Río de la Plata
PAMPAS
Santa Rosa
Olavarría
Tandil
Mar del Plata
Salado
Sierra Lihuel-Calel
Bahía Blanca
Necochea
Neuquen
Colorado
Negro
Bahía Blanca
Limay
L. Nahuel Huapí
Viedma
Golfo San Matias
Valdés Peninsula
Trelew
Rawson
Chubut
Comodoro Rivadavia
Golfo San Jorge
Caleta Olivia
L. Buenos Aires
Deseado
Cape Tres Puntas
PATAGONIA
ANDES
Puerto Santa Cruz
L. San Martín
L. Viedma
Bahia Grande
L. Argentino
Río Gallegos
Strait of Magellan
TIERRA DEL FUEGO
Isla de los Estados
Ushuaia
Beagle Channel
Cape Horn
N
Falkland Islands (Islas Malvinas) (administered by the UK; claimed by Argentina)
KEY
Cities and towns by population
over 1,000,000
over 500,000
over 200,000
over 100,000
under 100,000
Other symbols
high points
country border
0 100 200 300 400 500 600 miles
0 200 400 600 800 km

Argentina's largest lake is the salt Lake Mar Chiquita (546 sq. mi; 1,414 sq. km) in the province of Córdoba.

District, retreating glaciers have created hundreds of beautiful lakes, whose deep-blue waters reflect the surrounding mountains. The largest of these, Lake Nahuel Huapí, lies at an altitude of 2,516 feet (767 m).

At Argentina's northern border with Bolivia, the Andes divide into two parallel cordilleras, or mountain chains, the Salta-Jujeña to the west and the Sierra Subandina to the east. Between the cordilleras is a sparsely vegetated *altiplano*, or high plateau.

The Pampas and the Chaco

The word *pampa* is an old Quéchua Indian word meaning "plain" or "field." The grasslands of the Pampas cover most of the center of Argentina—a vast area of some 154,500 square miles (400,000 sq. km) that stretches in a radius of 600 miles (960 km) to the south, west, and north of Buenos Aires. The Pampas are divided into large cattle ranches, called *estancias,* and are home to gauchos, Argentina's cowboys (*see* p. 21).

ARGENTINA'S LANDFORMS

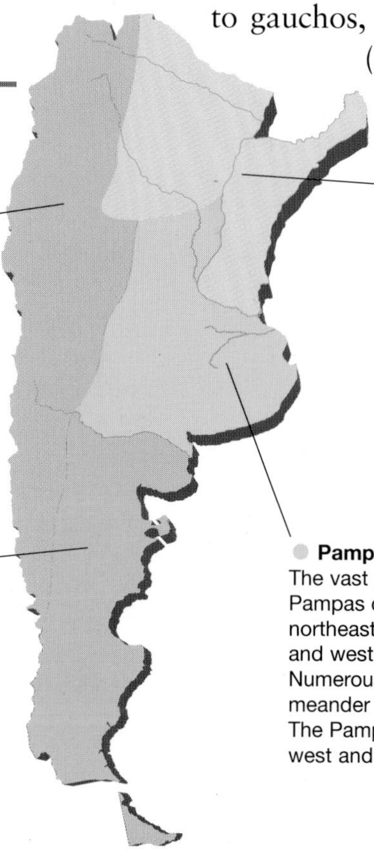

Glaciers and Glaciation

Glaciers are large, permanent masses of solid ice that form over thousands of years as winter snows accumulate and become compact. Eventually the weight of ice causes the glacier to move, slowly advancing and retreating according to the season and long-term climate change.

Sometimes glaciers are so huge that they cover an entire continent, as in Antarctica, and are called ice sheets. The Antarctic ice sheet, for example, covers some 5,500,000 square miles (14,245,000 sq. km).

Other glaciers form in high mountain ranges, such as the Himalayas and the Alps, and flow into the surrounding valleys and even onto the lowland.

The formation and movement of glaciers—glaciation—has helped shape the way the Earth's surface looks today. Until about 10,000 years ago, one-third of the Earth was covered with ice. Expanding and retreating glaciers cut out deep valleys and craggy peaks, polished the land until it was flat and smooth, or deposited large amounts of earth and stone called moraine.

Almost all of Patagonia was once covered with ice. The numerous lakes that today dot the landscape are the result of glaciation. A few mountain glaciers can still be seen. The spectacular Perito Moreno Glacier (above), at the southern tip of the Andes, is 31 miles (50 km) long and 2 miles (3 km) wide. It gets its name from the Argentine naturalist Francisco Moreno (1852–1919), who was one of the first Europeans to explore Patagonia.

Until recently, the Perito Moreno was one of the few glaciers in the world that was actually expanding. Periodically the glacier grew big enough to dam Lake Argentino, causing the lake's water level to rise. Eventually the pressure of the water caused the dam to collapse in a spectacular explosion of ice and water.

There are two different areas in the Pampas: the *pampa húmeda* ("humid pampas") and the *pampa seca* ("dry pampas"). Most of the country's important agricultural lands are on the humid pampas, to the east of Buenos Aires. The dry pampas lies farther west, toward the Andes.

The Argentine Chaco is also known as the Chaco Austral ("Southern Chaco") and covers 66,000 square miles (170,940 sq. km).

Northeastern Argentina is also lowland. From the vast estuary of the Río de la Plata, two of South America's mightiest rivers—the Paraná and the Uruguay—stretch northward. Between the rivers is a region of grasslands, marshes, and flooded forests known as Mesopotamia (Greek for "between the rivers"). To the west of Mesopotamia, across the Paraná, is the Chaco—a vast, dry plain that forms part of the much larger Gran Chaco that extends into Brazil, Bolivia, and Paraguay.

Patagonia and Tierra del Fuego

South of the Colorado River and stretching to the very tip of mainland Argentina at the Strait of Magellan are huge expanses of flat, barren tableland. This is Patagonia, which covers more than one-quarter of Argentina—some 311,000 square miles (805,490 sq. km). Its wild landscapes were among the last areas of the country to be explored and settled.

The wild and remote Tierra del Fuego, across the Strait of Magellan, is South America's largest island and the world's most southerly inhabited land.

Off the southernmost tip of Argentina is the island of Tierra del Fuego ("land of fire"), separated from the mainland by the Strait of Magellan. Argentina shares the island with Chile, which has the western section. Covering some 29,345 square miles (76,000 sq. km), the island is roughly the size of the state of South Carolina. Like Patagonia, Tierra del Fuego has both windy plains and mountains with glaciers and forests.

PROVINCES OF ARGENTINA

Argentina consists of 23 provinces, plus the federal district of Buenos Aires. In addition, Argentina also lays claim to two territories: the South Atlantic islands (*Islas del Atlántico Sur*), including the Islas Malvinas/Falkland Islands, South Georgia, and the South Sandwich islands—all of which are administered by the United Kingdom; and a segment of the Antarctica (*Antártida Argentina*). Below is a list of the provinces, together with their capitals, which are marked on the map with a dot.

BUENOS AIRES La Plata
CATAMARCA Catamarca
CHACO Resistencia
CHUBUT Rawson
CÓRDOBA Córdoba
CORRIENTES Corrientes
ENTRE RÍOS Paraná
FORMOSA Formosa
JUJUY San Salvador de Jujuy
LA PAMPA Santa Rosa
LA RIOJA La Rioja
MENDOZA Mendoza
MISIONES Posadas
NEUQUÉN Neuquén
RÍO NEGRO Viedma
SALTA Salta
SAN JUAN San Juan
SAN LUIS San Luis
SANTA CRUZ Río Gallegos
SANTA FE Santa Fe
SANTIAGO DEL ESTERO Santiago del Estero
TIERRA DEL FUEGO Ushuaia
TUCUMÁN San Miguel de Tucumán

ARGENTINA'S PROVINCES

Argentina is divided into 23 provinces, plus a federal capital—the capital city of Buenos Aires. Many of the provinces, such as Córdoba and Salta, grew up around old colonial cities from which they took their names. Others were formed later, as Argentina extended its territory southward across the steppes of Patagonia.

The Pampas Provinces

The provinces of Buenos Aires, La Pampa, Santa Fe, and Córdoba form the heartland of modern Argentina. Much of the provinces' territory is made up of the rich wheatfields and pasturelands of the Pampas. Buenos Aires is Argentina's largest, richest,

Buenos Aires province has a population of more than 12.5 million—4.5 times bigger than the next most populated province, Santa Fe.

and most populous province. It covers 118,843 square miles (307,805 sq. km), making it slightly larger in size than Arizona. Numerous highways and railroads crisscross the Pampas, connecting the province's many prosperous and attractive cities. The capital is the grandiose La Plata, which was founded in the 1880s after Buenos Aires became the federal capital.

To the north of Buenos Aires is another agricultural province, Santa Fe. The province grew up around the old colonial city of Santa Fe, which was built close to where the Salado River flows into the Paraná. Although the city remains the provincial capital, the port of Rosario downstream is today more important (*see* pp. 44–45).

La Pampa province—as its name suggests—consists almost entirely of flat grasslands, or pampas. In the south of the province, though, is a desert area of low, pinkish mountains that is home to a wealth of wildlife, including pumas and other wild cats. The area is today a national park—the Parque Nacional Lihué Calel. La Pampa's capital is Santa Rosa.

To the north of La Pampa is the province of Córdoba. In the south and east are pampas, but in the west is a system of mountain ranges called the Sierras de Córdoba. The highest peak, at 9,350 feet (2,850 m), is Mount Chamapquí. Five rivers—the Primero ("first"), Segundo ("second"), Tercero ("third"), Cuarto ("fourth"), and Quinto ("fifth")—flow down from the mountains. The province's beautiful old capital, Córdoba, stands on the banks of the Primero River.

The Paraná

At 3,030 miles (4,875 km), the mighty Paraná is South America's second-longest river. Its name is a Guaraní Indian word meaning "father of the rivers." The Paraná has its source in the confluence of two rivers in southeastern Brazil. For hundreds of miles, it flows along the Argentine–Paraguayan border before flowing southward to join the Uruguay River at the Río de la Plata estuary. The Argentine part of the river is an important transportation route, linking the northern provinces with Buenos Aires and the Atlantic. Many Argentine cities and ports—Santa Fe, Paraná, Corrientes, and Resistencia—are found along its banks.

Gauchos

With his capelike poncho and ornate silver-decorated belt over baggy trousers, the gaucho is one of the most recognizable symbols of Argentina—an Argentine equivalent of the North American cowboy. The gaucho is very proud, strong, and highly independent, which is how the Argentines like to think of their own country.

In the 18th and 19th centuries, gauchos ruled the Pampas. They were skilled horse riders and tended herds of cattle and lived a simple, independent life on the open prairie. When the huge *estancias* were created and the Pampas divided up, the gauchos found jobs on the cattle ranches and their free lifestyle came to an end. In 1872, the poet José Hernández wrote a long poem about life on the Pampas, *Martin Fierro* (*see* p. 94–95). Hernández did much to create today's romantic image of the gaucho and started a tradition of literature about the gauchos known as *literatura gauchesca* ("gaucho literature"). Gauchos still work on cattle *estancias*, but low wages and poor living conditions have driven many of them to find other work.

Mesopotamia: The Land between the Rivers

Between the Paraná and Uruguay rivers lie the provinces of Entre Ríos, Corrientes, and Misiones, which together make up the region of Mesopotamia. Each province has a different landscape and its own identity. The most southerly, Entre Ríos ("between the rivers"), has rich, rolling grasslands. Like Buenos Aires, its prosperity has traditionally depended on the export of beef and hides.

The Iguazú Falls

In the jungle of Misiones province, on the border with Brazil, are the Iguazú Falls. This spectacular natural feature includes 275 separate waterfalls, which drop a distance of 240 feet (60 m).

The most spectacular part of the falls is at the Garganta del Diablo ("Devil's Gorge"). Bright rainbows form in the sprays of water that rise up high into the air. At dusk, flocks of birds swoop through the misty spray on their way back to their nests.

The Indians tell a story about how the falls were created. A warrior named Caroba fell in love with a young girl named Naipur, who was also loved by the god of the forests. Together, Caroba and Naipur fled down the Iguazú River in a canoe. The angry god caused the riverbed to collapse before them, hurtling Naipur over the newly created falls. The girl was turned into a rock at their base, while Caroba became a tree hanging over the falls.

Today tourism is important, too, with visitors coming to fish its rivers or to camp in its shady forests. Entre Ríos's modern capital, Paraná, overlooks the river of the same name, opposite Santa Fe.

Corrientes province has grassy hills, marshlands, and, in the north, woodlands. Its capital, also called Corrientes, is one of Argentina's most beautiful old cities and is famous for its lively carnival.

Misiones, in the far north, is mountainous, with forests of pine and cedar trees. The province forms a peninsula of Argentine land, with Brazil to the east and Paraguay to the west. Misiones gets its name from the missionary settlements set up by Jesuit priests (*see* p. 56). One of the province's most famous sights is the spectacular Iguazú Falls, on the Iguazú River (*see* box opposite). The provincial capital is the river port of Posadas.

The Yatay Palm

Overlooking the bank of the Uruguay River in Argentina's Entre Ríos province is the small El Palmar National Park. The park is one of the few surviving habitats of the graceful yatay palm, which once grew throughout Uruguay, southern Brazil, and Argentine Mesopotamia. The introduction of the cattle to the region prevented the tree from reproducing because the livestock fed on the young seedlings. Today young yatay trees are able to grow only in protected areas.

The Andean Northwest

In the mountainous northwestern corner of Argentina are a cluster of provinces—Jujuy, Salta, Catamarca, Tucumán, La Rioja, and Santiago del Estero—that have more in common with Andean countries, such as Bolivia, Chile, and Peru, than with the rest of Argentina.

Before the arrival of the Spanish, this was the most populous region of the country. The native peoples grew corn and potatoes and, in the decades before the arrival of the Spanish, were governed by the powerful Inca people to the north. Even today, the Indian heritage is strong in the region. There are large communities of Quéchua Indians, and their influence is evident in the colorful weavings and pottery made in the region.

Jujuy (pronounced hoo-hooey) is said to have received its name from the title given to the local Inca governor—*Xuxuyoc* (hoo-hoo-ee-oc).

The tower and dome of Salta Cathedral dominate the skyline of this beautiful, old city founded in 1582.

The first cities of the region were founded by Spanish settlers from Bolivia and Peru who came across the Andes Mountains. Later, each city became the capital of a surrounding province. San Salvador de Jujuy stands in a high mountain valley and has a mild, springlike climate all year round. Santiago del Estero, Argentina's oldest city, is capital of its namesake province. San Miguel de Tucumán, capital of Argentina's smallest province, Tucumán, is the home of the country's sugar industry. Beautiful Salta is situated in a lush river valley high up in the mountains.

In the south of the region, La Rioja and Catamarca are among Argentina's remotest and poorest provinces. However, they are also among its most beautiful. There are high mountains, dark forests, and lowlands planted with orange trees, vines, and figs.

The Chaco Provinces

The provinces of Chaco and Formosa include the bulk of the desolate, hot lowlands of savanna and dense thorn forest known as the Chaco. The people here traditionally depended on forestry to make their living. The red quebracho tree, found only in the Chaco, is a rich source of tannin, which is used in the process of tanning leather. Today, though, the forests are gradually being cleared to make way for crops such as cotton and sunflowers.

Asunción, the capital of Paraguay, lies just across the border from Formosa province.

The population is small, and there are very few roads. Most people live in the provincial capitals. Resistencia, the capital of Chaco, stands on the Paraná River opposite Corrientes and is famous for the many sculptures and statues that grace its streets. Formosa, capital of its namesake province, is a busy port on the Paraguay River.

Cuyo: Sunshine and Wine

Together, the provinces of Mendoza, San Juan, and San Luis have their own special character and are sometimes known collectively as the Cuyo. The Cuyo gets its name from the region's sandy earth, which was called *cuyum* in the local Indian language. To the west are the soaring Andes, whose melting snows create the numerous rivers that water this otherwise dry region. The rivers, helped by extensive artificial irrigation systems, support a flourishing agricultural landscape of vineyards and olive groves.

Bustling Mendoza is Cuyo's most important city. Its avenues are lined with trees that are watered by a system of irrigation canals. The city is the center of the Argentine wine production. Every February, the people of Mendoza celebrate the end of the wine harvest with a lively festival.

The other provincial capitals are much smaller than Mendoza. After a devastating earthquake in 1944, San Juan's downtown had to be entirely rebuilt. The inhabitants like to keep their rebuilt city very clean. San Luis is a small, industrial city.

Wine Cultivation

Spanish missionaries were the first to plant grapevines in Mendoza. Wine production began to flourish only in the late 18th century, when French and Italian immigrants settled in the region. Argentina is now the world's fifth-largest wine producer and is well known for its high-quality red wines. Since 1913, Mendoza has hosted the *Fiesta Nacional de la Vendimia,* an annual, week-long wine festival held at the end of February. The festival attracts people from all over the province. There are concerts and a parade of floats along Avenida San Martín, the city's main street. The fiesta ends with the coronation of a festival queen. The *mendocinos* (people of Mendoza) call their home *La Tierra del Sol y Buen Vino*—"the land of sun and good wine."

The Patagonian Provinces

The name *Patagonia* is often applied to the whole of the southern tip of South America, including parts of both Argentina and Chile. No one is quite sure where the name comes from. One account suggests that the word derives from the name that the first Spanish explorers gave the

A bus journeys toward the spectacular Fitzroy Mountains in remote Santa Cruz province. The highest peak in the range, Cerro Fitzroy, also known as Chaltel, rises to 11,070 feet (3,374 m).

The province of Chubut gets its name from an Indian word meaning "meandering river."

region's native peoples (*see* pp. 50–51). They called them *Patagones* because of their large, moccasined feet—*pata* means "foot" or "paw" in Spanish.

Argentine Patagonia comprises the provinces of Río Negro, Neuquén, Chubut, and Santa Cruz. The Argentine government settled the region only in the 19th century, ruthlessly exterminating the native peoples. Even today, this region is thinly populated and settlements can be hundreds of miles apart. Much of the Patagonian plains are divided into vast sheep-ranching *estancias*. The houses of the gaucho workers often cluster around a central ranch house.

Every year, thousands of tourists come to this beautiful region to walk, climb, and ski. Especially popular is the Lake District, which stretches along the foot of the Andes in Neuquén, Río Negro, and Chubut provinces. Here, beech forests skirt snow-capped mountains and deep-blue lakes. The area is also home to several large national parks (*see* p. 33). The town of San Carlos de Bariloche in Río Negro grew spectacularly in the late 20th century in the wake of the massive tourist boom.

Most of the region's big cities are found along Patagonia's east coast with its fertile river valleys. The lively, modern city of Viedma—Río Negro's capital—stands at the mouth of the Río Negro ("Black River"), after which the province is named. Farther south is the port of Rawson, the capital of Chubut province. Chubut's first European settlers were Welsh colonists who came to Argentina in the 19th century (*see* box). They named Rawson after the Argentine minister who granted them the land.

The capital of Patagonia's most southerly province, Santa Cruz, is the port of Río Gallegos—an important center for the wool trade and for the nearby oil- and coalfields. In summer, tourists come to visit the Perito Moreno Glacier and the slopes of the craggy Fitzroy Mountains.

Tierra del Fuego

The wild, remote province of Tierra del Fuego ("Land of Fire") is made up of the eastern half of the Isla Grande ("Big Island") together with a few nearby islands. The western half of the island belongs to Chile.

On the north of the island, overlooking the Strait of Magellan, are windswept plains, grazed by thousands of sheep.

"Little Wales"

The only Welsh community outside Wales is in Trelew, Chubut province, and in the surrounding towns and villages, such as Gaiman, Trevelin, and Dolavon. The original settlers followed a church minister, Michael D. Jones, from Wales to Patagonia in 1865. Jones wanted to create a "little Wales beyond Wales," where his people would be free from the influence and power of the English. Speaking the Welsh language and having the right to worship in their chapels were particularly important for the founding members of the community. The city of Trelew got its name from another Welshman, Lewis Jones: *Tre* is Welsh for "town," while *lew* is short for Lewis.

Today the Welsh language is dying in Argentina; younger people prefer to speak Spanish. The country's Welsh communities rely largely on tourism to make a living. Tourists come to visit the red-brick chapels, to eat in the tea houses, or to watch the annual Welsh poetry festival (*Eisteddfod*).

Islas Malvinas or the Falkland Islands?

The windswept Islas Malvinas lie some 300 miles (480 km) northeast of the tip of Argentina. The islands were first settled in 1764 by the French, who named them after the port of St.-Malo. In 1765, the British also settled on the islands. They called them the Falkland Islands after a British naval officer named Viscount Falkland.

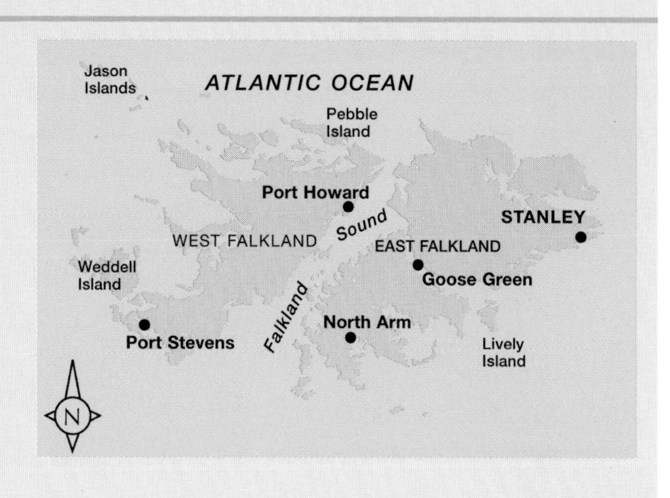

The Spanish also claimed the islands for their empire under the terms of the Treaty of Tordesillas (*see* p. 53). They bought the French settlement, and in 1770, they drove the British from the islands. When Argentina gained its independence in 1816, it also declared its sovereignty over the Malvinas. In the early 1830s, the United States and the British expelled the Spanish from the islands, and Britain founded a colony. By 1900, some 2,000 British settlers lived on the islands, making their living from sheep farming. The Argentine government protested against what they saw as the occupation of the Malvinas. The dispute reached a climax in 1982, when Argentina invaded the islands and the South Atlantic War broke out (*see* p. 73).

There are two main islands: East and West Falkland. The islands are mostly treeless grass- and scrubland, grazed by thousands of sheep. There are no native land mammals, but the surrounding seas are rich with marine mammals,including sea lions, dolphins, porpoises, and seals.

The islands' capital is Stanley. The islanders still live by sheep farming, producing thousands of tons of wool per year. Until the South Atlantic War, the Falklanders enjoyed friendly relations with their neighbors in Argentina.

On the southern coast are spectacular mountains and glaciers. To the south of Tierra del Fuego lies the icy Drake Passage and, beyond, Antarctica.

Despite its position in the far south, the province has a mild climate. Winter days are very short—as little as seven hours long—while summer days are very long, with 17.5 hours of daylight at the summer solstice. The provincial capital is Ushuaia (*see* pp. 46–47), which its inhabitants claim as the world's most southerly city.

CLIMATE

Most of Argentina lies south of the Tropic of Capricorn. Because Argentina lies in the Southern Hemisphere, summer is at the same time as North America's winter, and vice versa.

Argentina's great size and geographical diversity mean that it has an extremely varied climate. The north is subtropical, and temperatures can reach 104°F (40°C) between December and February, the Argentine summer. In the Pampas, the climate is mild and excellent for farming. The exception is the capital city, which can be extremely humid in the summer, with temperatures of 95°F (35°C). Patagonia, in the south, is flat and windy, and it is unusual for temperatures to rise above 68°F (20°C).

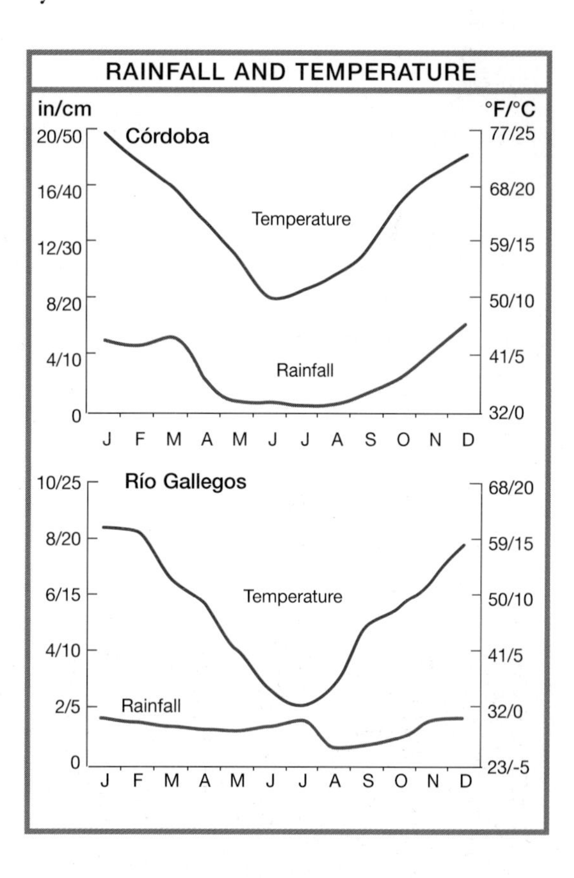

Córdoba in the north has wet, hot summers and cold, dry winters. Río Gallegos in the far south is cool and dry all year round.

A strong, dry, hot wind known as the Zonda sometimes blows down from the Andes and across the Pampas, causing a sudden, dramatic increase in temperature. The wind blows away the dust, making it easy to see long distances. The disadvantage, Argentines say, is that the wind causes headaches and bad moods.

The mighty Andean condor is a member of the vulture family. Its wingspan can measure more than 10 feet (3 m), enabling it to soar at very high altitudes. Condors build their nests some 10,000 feet (3,000 m) up in the mountains.

ANIMALS AND PLANTS

Because Argentina's population is small and concentrated in large cities such as Buenos Aires, there is plenty of room for wildlife to flourish. The astonishing diversity of Argentina's native plants and animals reflects the wide variety of natural environments that the country provides. There are subtropical rain forests and bushy steppes; mountain grasslands and sandy coastlines; cool evergreen forests and dry, hot deserts.

Under the Forest Canopy, Over the Mountains

The warm, wet subtropical forests of the far northeast have a rich plantlife. Giant trees such as the Misiones cedar and the *palo rosa* tower over bamboos, figs, and tree ferns. Vines, liana, and bright orchids wind themselves about the trees, and the forest floor is a tangle of ferns and the green herb *yerba mate* (*see* p. 108). The forests are home to jaguars, monkeys, and the racoonlike coatimundi. Jewel-colored toucans, parrots, and parakeets flutter beneath the high forest canopy, filling the air with their cries.

In the Andes, condors soar high up in the sky, and wildcats and pumas hunt in the mountain forests. A lucky visitor might catch a glimpse of the tiny deer named the *pudú*, which today is an endangered species. Plentiful salmon and trout, of which some specimens can weigh as much as 35 pounds (16 kg), live in the many lakes of the Argentine Lake District. In summer, the alpine meadows are carpeted with flowers.

The tall, reedlike pampas grass, with its silvery flowers, is only one of the many grasses found in the Pampas.

On the Pampas

Over the centuries, the landscape of the Pampas has changed dramatically. The native peoples who once hunted here frequently burned the bushland to flush out their prey, which favored the growth of juicy grasses. The European colonists also brought new plants, which often escaped into the wild. European thistles and artichokes, for example, spread rapidly across the Pampas, overwhelming native species. The lush grasses also enabled extensive cattle grazing, which had a profound impact on the landscape.

The lack of variety in natural habitat in the Pampas means that few animal species live there. Of these, the most distinctive is the vizcacha, a gray, whiskered rodent that can weigh as much as 20 pounds (9 kg). The Pampas' lakes and lagoons, however, are home to a rich variety of birdlife, including black-necked swans, storks, flamingos, and ibis. The flightless rhea, which was once caught in large numbers by the Indians of the Pampas, is today a rare sight on the grasslands.

The Ombú Tree

One of the most remarkable sights of the Pampas is the huge, spreading *ombú* tree. The tree can grow as tall as 65 feet (19.5 m), with branches spreading more than 100 feet (30 m). The tree is not native to the landscape, which was originally treeless. European settlers introduced the *ombú* from Mesopotamia to provide shelter from the hot, midday sun. The tree's very name means shade in the Guaraní language. There is a famous *ombú* tree in the Plaza San Martín in Buenos Aires.

Wildlife of the Sea

Some of Argentina's most interesting wildlife is found off the coast in the Atlantic Ocean. The waters off the Patagonian coast and Tierra del Fuego are home to

A penguin sits on its nest among a large colony on the Patagonian seashore.

Guanaco

The guanaco is a large mammal of the camel family that lives in small herds on the Pampas and mountain plateaus. Native to South America, the guanaco is an ancestor of the llama. Sandy-brown in color, it has a black face and soft wool and grows to about 4 feet (1.2 m) tall. Its body is about 5 feet (1.5 m) long. Hunted by native peoples for its meat and wool (left), the number of guanacos has been seriously reduced. Today the animal is on CITES's threatened species list.

killer and southern right whales. The killer whales arrive between March and May, timing their arrival to prey on the young of sea lions, which breed a couple of months earlier. The southern right whales, which arrive later in June, stay off the Argentine coast until December, when they travel farther south looking for food. Penguins and seals also live and breed in the sheltered gulfs along the coastline.

Argentina's endangered species include:

- **Andean condor**
- **giant armadillo**
- **humpback, blue, southern right, and sperm whales**
- ***pudú***
- **Darwin's Rhea**

Endangered Species

While Argentines are aware of the need to protect the environment, the rivers and the air, particularly around Buenos Aires, are still being polluted. In the northern rain forests, large areas of trees have been felled by timber companies, while river environments are being altered by hydroelectric projects. As a consequence, a large number of Argentine animals are in danger of extinction or are threatened and are listed under the Convention on International Trade in Endangered Species (CITES).

National Parks

Argentina has created a large network of national parks to protect its plants and animals. The oldest national park, Nahuel Huapí, in the Andean Lake District, was set up in 1934. Today there are 19 national parks, situated throughout the country.

The national parks vary widely in size and terrain. The vast Nahuel Huapí National Park covers some 2,880 square miles (7,460 sq. km) and features spectacular peaks and glaciers. The park attracts thousands of visitors every year, but few of them manage to spot one if its rarest sights, the tiny *pudú* deer. At the other end of the scale is the tiny El Palmar National Park, on the bank of the Uruguay River (*see* p. 23).

Other areas have been designated Natural Monuments and Natural Reserves. In Patagonia is the Monumento Natural Bosques Petrificados, whose natural wonder is its strange, fossilized trees. Some 150 million years ago, volcanic activity flattened the forests of the area and buried them with ash. Later, erosion of the rock that formed round the trees exposed the trees' petrified forms. By contrast, the natural wonder of the Reserva Faunística Península Valdés in Patagonia is the wildlife that lives on its shores and headlands—including sea lions, seals, and penguins.

The spectacular Fitzroy Mountains (shown left) are a dramatic feature of the Los Glaciares National Park.

Argentines claim that the Avenida 9 de Julio ("Avenue of July 9") in Buenos Aires is the world's widest street. From curb to curb, it is 460 feet (140 m) wide. Along its length are the massive, dark-green trees known as palo borrachos.

BUENOS AIRES

Argentina is dominated by its capital city, Buenos Aires. It is the home of the national government and much of the country's industry and business. More than a third of the country's 35 million inhabitants live in the Greater Buenos Aires area, which includes the capital city itself and its vast suburbs. The population distribution of Argentina is so uneven that the city with the second-largest number of people in the country is Córdoba, which has only 1.2 million inhabitants. The inhabitants of Buenos Aires are called *porteños*, which means "people of the port."

The "Port of Good Winds"

The city stands on the bank of the Río de la Plata ("Silver River"), which in English is called the Plate River. The Plate is not really a river at all but a huge, muddy estuary, or river mouth, some 186 miles (300 km) long and, where it enters the Atlantic Ocean, 136 miles (220 km) wide. Farther upstream, the estuary becomes the Paraná and Uruguay rivers. On the opposite bank of the Río de la Plata is Montevideo, the capital of Uruguay.

In the 16th century, the Spanish explorers who founded the city gave it the grandiose name of Puerto Nuestra Señora Santa María del Buen Aire—the "Port of Our Lady of Good Winds." Santa María del Buen Aire was a title of the Virgin Mary, to whom sailors prayed for a speedy voyage. Over time, this long name was shortened to Buenos Aires. Many people, though, supposed that the city got its name because of the pure, clear air that the Spanish found around the estuary.

Street Names

The important streets and avenues of Argentina's cities are named after the great events and people of the country's history. Almost every city, for example, has an Avenida Independencia ("Avenue of Independence"), and there are usually streets named after the heroes of independence, such as San Martín and Belgrano. Other dates remembered are May 25, the date of the revolution in Buenos Aires, and July 9, marking the declaration of independence at Tucumán. Some streets are named after great 19th-century presidents, such as Sarmiento and Mitre. Few, however, have been named after Juan and Evita Perón.

The *Barrios*

Like New York, Buenos Aires is a city of immigrants. During the 19th century, thousands of Europeans from Spain, Italy, England, and Ukraine arrived in the port in search of work and a better life. Different nationalities settled in different neighborhoods, called *barrios*, where they lived and worked. Every *barrio* had its own church, where locals worshiped, and a plaza, or square, where they met, drank and ate, and gossiped. *Porteños* are very proud of the *barrio* in which they grew up. They support their native *barrio*'s soccer team and sing the local tango songs.

The most famous *barrio* is La Boca, on the southeastern tip of the city. La Boca stands on the site of the first Spanish settlement at Buenos Aires. In the 19th century,

La Boca is famous for its multicolored corrugated-iron buildings. The houses were first painted this way by Italian immigrants, who missed the warm, sunny colors of their home country.

THE BARRIOS

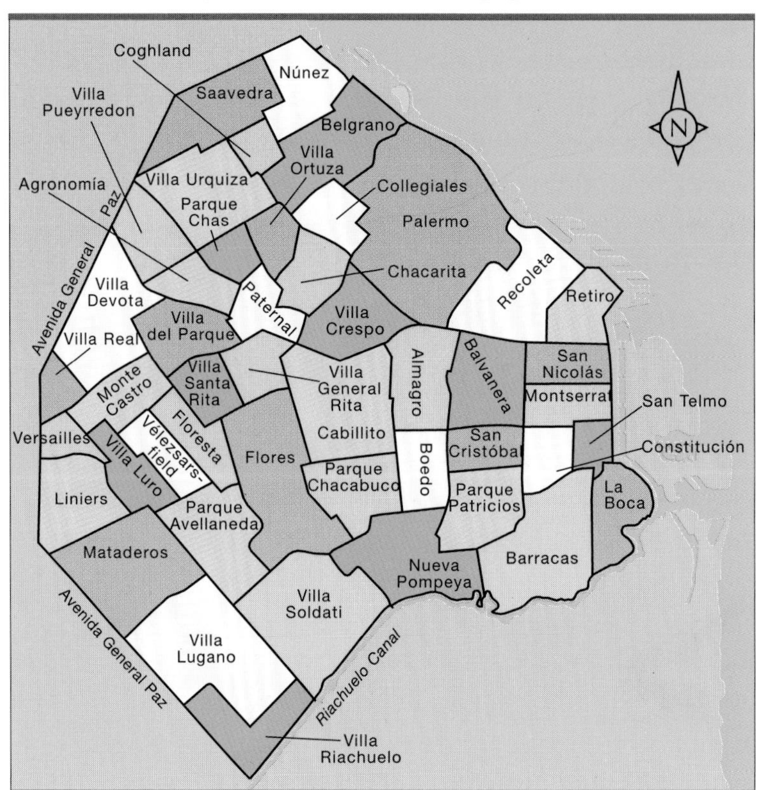

*The boundaries of the Federal Capital (***Capital Federal***) are marked by the Avenida ("***avenue***") General Paz and the Riachuelo Canal. The capital is really a collection of neighborhoods, or* ***barrios****, each of which has its own special character.*

factories and warehouses were built along the Riachuelo Canal, which runs through the neighborhood, and La Boca became a bustling dock area. Italian sailors and dock and factory workers settled in the area and built their houses out of materials from abandoned ships. The facades were made out of corrugated iron and painted in bright colors. La Boca is the traditional home of tango.

The *barrio* of Villa Crespo is the traditional Jewish neighborhood of Buenos Aires. The city's Jewish community of some 250,000 people is one of the largest in South America. Other *barrios* are home to the wealthy. Palermo, for example, is famous for its grand, Italian-style villas and polo field. The *barrio* of San Telmo, once infamous for its cramped, crumbling apartment buildings, is now being given a facelift. The northern *barrio* of Belgrano has many museums.

The *barrio* Palermo gets its name not from the city in Sicily but from Juan Domínguez Palermo, who owned the area in the 17th century.

Around the City

The British naturalist Charles Darwin (*see* pp. 64–65) visited Buenos Aires in 1833. He thought the city "one of the most regular in the world. Every street is at right angles to the one it crosses, and the parallel ones being equidistant [at an equal distance], the houses are collected into solid squares of equal dimensions, which are called *cuadras*." Buenos Aires's downtown is still laid out on a grid system, with its focus the beautiful Plaza de Mayo, so it is easy for visitors to get their bearings.

The best way of seeing the sights of Buenos Aires is on foot. The city is full of cafés that make convenient resting points, and *porteños* spend hours in them drinking coffee, meeting friends, or chatting. Buenos Aires has a reliable and efficient public transport system. *Colectivos* are buses that travel all over the city. They are very small, and tall people need to bend over to see out of windows. The subway system, the Subte, is the oldest in South America and dates from 1913. The

The word *Subte* is short for *subterráneo,* Spanish for "underground" or "subway."

BUENOS AIRES METRO—THE SUBTE

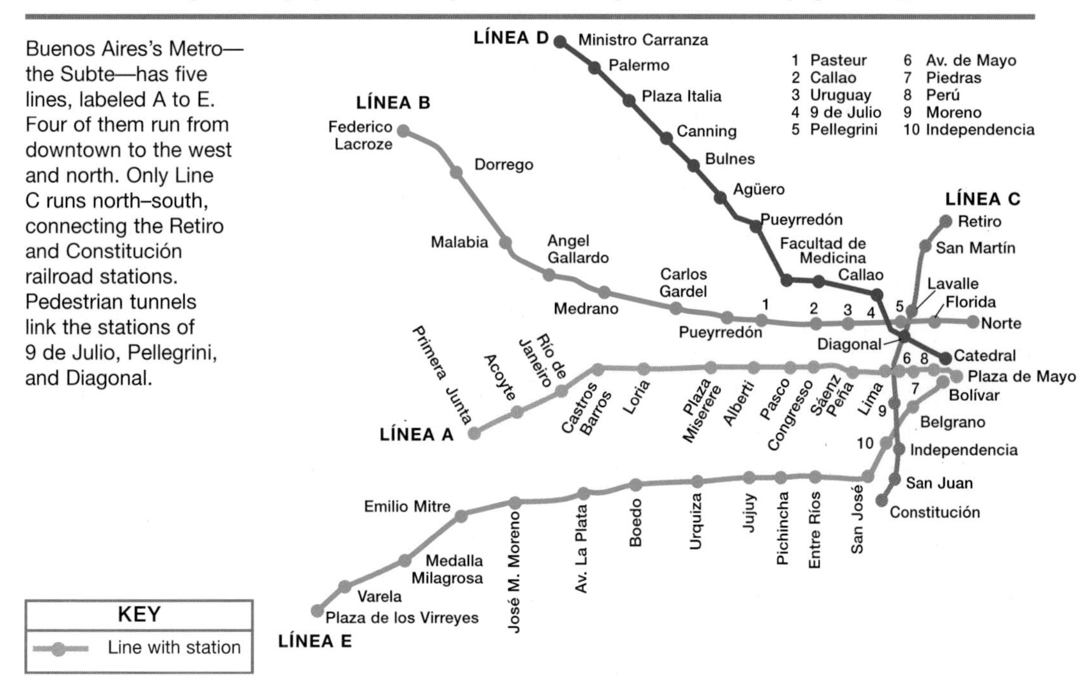

Buenos Aires's Metro—the Subte—has five lines, labeled A to E. Four of them run from downtown to the west and north. Only Line C runs north–south, connecting the Retiro and Constitución railroad stations. Pedestrian tunnels link the stations of 9 de Julio, Pellegrini, and Diagonal.

oldest Subte route, Line A, starts at the Plaza de Mayo. It still has the original wood-trimmed trains, and its stations are decorated with beautiful ceramic tiles.

Taxis are easily identified by their black and yellow colors. They are inexpensive and plentiful, except in a heavy rainstorm when everyone seems to want one. Ferries and hydrofoils cross the Río de la Plata to Montevideo. Despite all these transportation options, many people still travel into the city by automobile. Traffic jams often clog the city's wide boulevards and narrow streets.

The Plaza de Mayo

The heart of Buenos Aires is the Plaza de Mayo, which lies at the city's eastern edge, close to the Río de la Plata. A plaza has existed on the site since the city was founded in 1580. The plaza takes its name from May, the month during which the revolution of 1810 took place.

The rose-colored plaza is beautifully laid out with tall palm trees, elaborate flower gardens, and monuments. Bordering the square are some of the country's most important buildings. On the north side is the grand Catedral Metropolitana, the Roman

DOWNTOWN BUENOS AIRES

Buenos Aires's downtown is focused on the *barrios* of San Nicolás and Montserrat. Its heart is the Plaza de Mayo, which lies just inland from the city's docks. Around the plaza are many of the city's key buildings—the cathedral, city hall (*cabildo*), and presidential palace. Like most Spanish colonial cities, the downtown is based on a grid plan. Broad, tree-lined avenues—*avenidas*—crisscross through the city.

At the center of the palm-tree lined Plaza de Mayo is the Pirámide de Mayo ("Pyramid of May"), a monument commemorating the 1810 Revolution. Beyond the pyramid is the pink facade of the Casa Rosada.

Catholic cathedral, built on the site of the first church in Buenos Aires. Inside the cathedral is the tomb of Argentina's greatest national hero, José de San Martín (1778–1850; *see* pp. 61–62).

On the east side of the plaza is the presidential palace, the Casa Rosada ("pink house"), which is named for its rose-colored exterior. The balcony of the Casa Rosada has been the scene of many key moments in Argentina's history. Traditionally, after a president takes office, he or she stands on the balcony to address the people.

On the opposite side of the square from the Casa Rosada is the Cabildo (city hall). The Cabildo once spanned the whole western edge of the square, but today it is much smaller. Inside the Cabildo is a museum that tells the history of Argentina.

In times of celebration or crisis, the plaza has often been a rallying point for the Argentine people. In May 1810, people gathered there to celebrate their nation's independence from Spain. In 1982, they rallied to show their support for General Galtieri's invasion of the Malvinas/Falklands. Four years later, thousands gathered to celebrate Argentina's victory in the World Cup soccer championships. The most famous demonstrators of the plaza are the Mothers of the Plaza de Mayo. Every

Visitors to the Teatro Colón have to crane their necks to see the painted ceiling of its spectacular auditorium. Seven tiers of seats rise above the audience in the orchestra.

Thursday afternoon they come to protest about their "disappeared children," murdered during the military dictatorships of the 1970s.

Running east–west from the plaza is the Avenida de Mayo (Avenue of May). Crossing the Avenida de Mayo is the Avenida 9 de Julio (*see* p. 34). Measuring 460 feet (140 m) from sidewalk to sidewalk, this is the broadest avenue in the world, and it is always busy with traffic. In the middle of the Avenida 9 de Julio is the Obelisco, which stands almost 230 feet high (70 m). It was built in 1936 to commemorate the 400th anniversary of the city's founding. Three years after it was built, the city council voted to have it pulled down as an eyesore, but it still stands today. Just off the huge avenue are narrow streets that have changed little since colonial times.

Theaters and Museums

The main auditorium of the Teatro Colón can seat an audience of more than 3,500.

Porteños love culture, and Buenos Aires has a large number of theaters, movies, and museums. The most famous is the opera house, Teatro Colón, named for Christopher Columbus, who is known as Cristóbal Colón in Spanish. The Teatro Colón is so big that it occupies a whole block off the Avenida 9 de Julio. The interior has huge colored-glass domes, and the main auditorium is seven stories high. The theater houses not only the opera but also the National Symphony Orchestra and the National Ballet. The *barrio* of San Telmo is a major museum district of Buenos Aires, as is the Recoleta *barrio*, which is home to the National Library and the city's chief museum, the *Museo Nacional de Bellas Artes*—the Museum of Fine Arts.

Famous Cemeteries

The Recoleta barrio is also famous for its cemetery. The Recoleta Cemetery is one of the most famous burial places in the world. The city's rich have their last resting place in elaborately decorated tombs—including pyramids and ancient Greek-style temples— that are laid out like a small grid-plan city with its own "streets" and "blocks." Around 70 of the mausoleums are today national monuments.

Recoleta's fame is mainly due to the fact that Argentina's most venerated figure, Eva Perón—the wife of President Juan Perón, most often known simply as "Evita"—is buried there (*see* p. 71). Perón himself is buried in the less exclusive cemetery of La Chacarita, which also holds the grave of the well-known tango singer Carlos Gardel (*see* p. 102).

> **"It is cheaper to live extravagantly all your life than to be buried in Recoleta."**
> **Argentine saying**

The cemetery of La Recoleta is a vast necropolis, or "city of the dead." Only the rich can afford to be buried here, commemorated by elaborate tombs and sculptures.

There are two cities in Latin America called Córdoba—one in Mexico and one in Argentina. Both are named after an older city in Spain.

BEYOND BUENOS AIRES

Although Buenos Aires is by far the most important city in Argentina, provincial cities such as Córdoba and Rosario play a large role in the nation's life.

Córdoba: Buenos Aires's Rival

The city of Córdoba lies at the heart of Argentina, in a fertile agricultural region between the Andes and the Pampas. It lies at the foot of the Sierra Chica on the Primero River, which runs east from the Córdoba Mountains to a large salt lake, Lake Mar Chiquita.

One of Córdoba's oldest buildings is its university. The National University of Córdoba was founded as a religious college in 1613.

Before the arrival of the Spanish, the area was inhabited by the Comechingones Indians, who grew corn and herded llamas. The Comechingones were also good warriors, and for a time, they were able to resist the Spanish invaders. Eventually, in 1573, the victorious Spanish were able to found a city in the region. They set about converting the Indians and made them work in the fields. The native population, however, was quickly killed by the new diseases that the Spanish brought with them.

In the 17th century, Córdoba was the most important city in Argentina. Its economy flourished, beautiful churches and other public buildings were built, and a university was founded. After the focus of Argentina shifted to Buenos Aires, the city went into decline. Its people, however, still saw their city as a rival to the port city. When Buenos Aires led the way in fighting for Argentina's independence, Córdoba rallied to the Spanish king, who at that time ruled the country.

Today the city is an important industrial center and is home to Argentina's automobile industry. Its people continue to challenge the supremacy of Buenos Aires. Córdoba's bustling, built-up downtown centers on the Plaza San Martín. Many of the buildings date from the city's heyday in the 17th and 18th centuries. Overlooking the square is the domed Iglesia Catedral, in which some of Argentina's most venerated heroes lie buried. The nearby historical museum is a jumble of different things, from musical instruments and religious paintings to weapons used by the Indian people.

After a hard day's work in a downtown office or in one of the factories that lie to the north of the river, the city's inhabitants like to relax in one of the large city parks. On weekends, they may explore the surrounding mountains, or sierras, by bike or go climbing.

Córdoba has a colorful calendar of festivals. In April, there is a huge crafts fair. On July 6, there are celebrations to mark the foundation of the city, and in September, there is a book fair attended by authors from all over the country.

Córdoba is a pleasant city to stroll through. Many of the streets around its old historic quarter are reserved for pedestrians only.

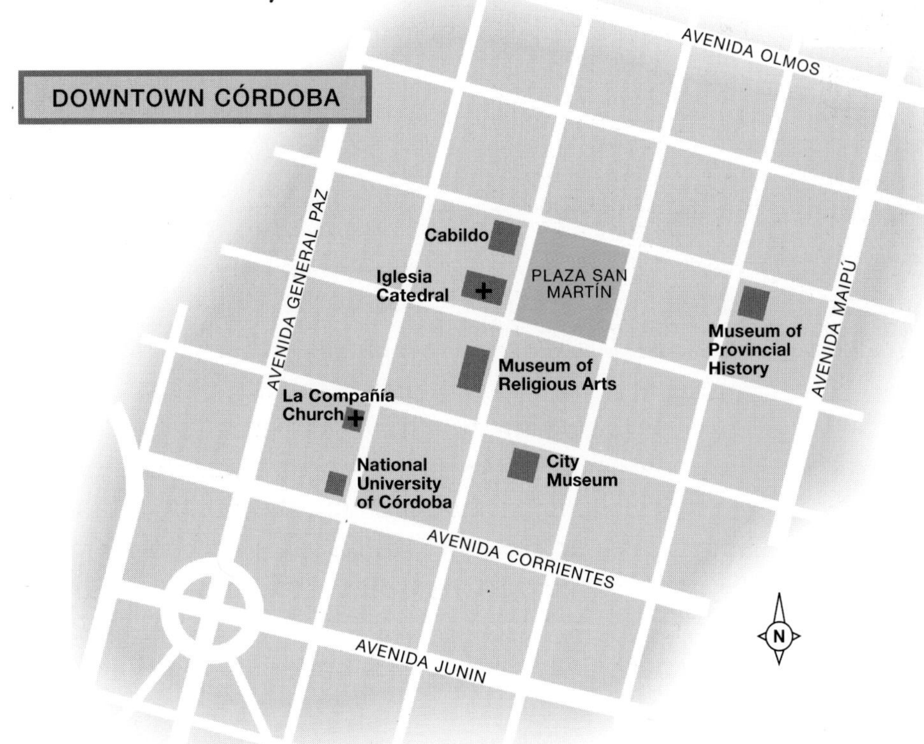

The inhabitants of Rosario are called *rosarinos.*

Rosario: "Cradle of the Flag"

Some 200 miles (320 km) upstream from Buenos Aires on the broad Paraná River is the industrial port of Rosario, once Argentina's capital. Once it was an even more important port than Buenos Aires. Oceangoing ships docked easily in its port, where they were loaded with the agricultural produce of the surrounding pampas as well as with the goods made in the city's factories. For this reason Rosario was sometimes called the "Chicago of Argentina." Today, however, Rosario is no longer as busy as it once was, and ships can be seen in its docks only rarely.

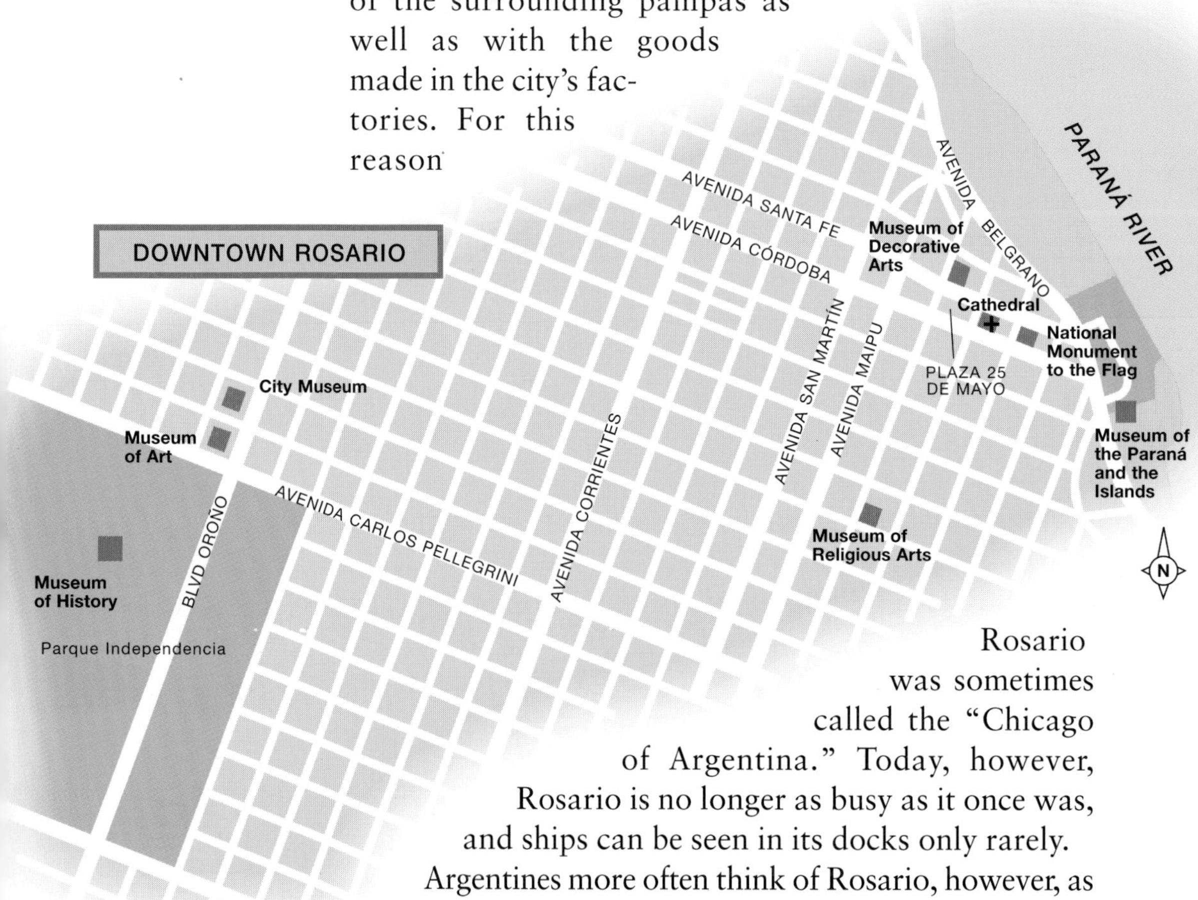

Argentines more often think of Rosario, however, as the home of their national flag and call the city "*la Cuna de la Bandera*"—"the cradle of the flag." Every June, the inhabitants—the *rosarinos*—celebrate Flag Week, which climaxes with the anniversary of the death of General Manuel Belgrano, who designed the flag.

Rosario is built on a very regular grid pattern overlooking the Paraná River. Its avenues are lined with shady palms.

Like Chicago, the city is based on a grid plan. In the downtown, long, tree-lined avenues are overlooked by elegant, French-style buildings as well as modern apartment houses. There are large, shady squares and numerous leafy parks where the *rosarinos* like to stroll on hot days. The focus of the downtown is the Plaza 25 de Mayo and the nearby pedestrian shopping streets. Along the waterfront are numerous restaurants and cafés that have spectacular views across the river. On weekends, pleasure boats ferry passengers to and from the islands that dot the Paraná River.

Patriotic Argentines visit Rosario to see the huge National Monument to the Flag. This boat-shaped building shelters the tomb of General Belgrano and is topped by a 255 feet (78 m) "mast." The monument also houses a museum, where the first Argentine flag is on display. Rosario has other museums as well. The Museum of the Paraná and the Islands is decorated with beautiful murals showing the legends and history of this great waterway.

Santiago del Estero: "Mother of Cities"

In the hot, dry plains of northwest Argentina, between the Chaco and the Andes, is Santiago del Estero. Spanish settlers founded the city some 450 years ago, making it the oldest European settlement in what is today Argentina. For this reason, the city is known as the *Madre de Ciudades*—"Mother of Cities."

The city is the center for the surrounding agricultural region, with its vast fields of grain, cotton, and flax. The Dulce ("sweet") River flows through the region but does not supply the land with a dependable water supply. Sometimes the river is dry; other times it floods. Crops are often planted in the wake of floods.

Quilmes: An Indian City

Before the arrival of the Spanish in Argentina, few of its Indian inhabitants lived in permanent settlements. They led a nomadic (wandering) existence, hunting game and gathering wild foods. Only in the far north of the country were there villages and towns. The biggest Indian settlement was Quilmes, in present-day Tucumán province. The city was built a thousand years ago, and, at its height, was home to some 5,000 people. It had mighty walls and buildings, but was not strong enough to resist the Spanish, who laid siege to the city in 1667. Today Quilmes lies in ruins.

The city of Ushuaia lies at 54°47′ South—making it the world's most southern city.

Ushuaia: At the End of the World

On the wild and beautiful southern coast of Tierra del Fuego, at the very tip of Argentina, is the remote city of Ushuaia. The city lies just under 2,000 miles (3,200 km) by road from the capital, Buenos Aires, and is famous as the world's southernmost city. A spectacular landscape of dense beech forests and jagged, ice-covered peaks surrounds the city.

The Spanish and then the Argentines ignored this remote wilderness, and the local Yagán Indians lived here undisturbed for centuries. At first, the only Europeans to visit the area were those interested in its wildlife. The famous British naturalist Charles Darwin came here in 1834 (*see* pp. 64–65), and his ship, the *Beagle*, is remembered in the name of the sea channel at Tierra del Fuego's southern edge. In 1870, British missionary Thomas Bridges founded a settlement at Ushuaia and began to convert the Yagán to Christianity.

Later the Argentine government imprisoned hardened criminals and political prisoners in Ushuaia and on the even more remote Islas de los Estados. The city

The remote city of Ushuaia is home to some 42,000 people. Most of these have settled there only in the last 20 years.

began to grow only in the 1950s when it became a base for the Argentine navy. The government wanted to assert its claim to Antarctic territories that lie to the south. Today the population of some 42,000 lives by fishing, food processing, and especially tourism.

Unlike most cities in Argentina, Ushuaia is not built around a central plaza. Instead the downtown is formed by two avenues. Most of Ushuaia's shops, hotels, and banks are on the Avenida San Martín, while the Avenida Maipú overlooks the city's sheltered harbor.

Most of Ushuaia's downtown is formed by a couple of avenues near the town's sheltered harbor. There is not much to see in Ushuaia itself. The old prison is now open to tourists and has 380 tiny cells, into which up to 600 inmates were squeezed at any one time. There is also the *Museo Territorial Fin del Mundo* (Regional Museum of the End of the World), which has displays on local wildlife and history, together with a "rogues gallery" of some of the notorious inmates once held in the prison.

Most people come to Ushuaia to explore the region's magnificent mountain landscapes. They can hike in the Tierra del Fuego National Park or go skiing or mountain biking. They can take boat trips to nearby islands to watch the wildlife—Isla de los Lobos has a colony of sea lions, while Isla de los Pájaros is home to thousands of birds. There are longer trips that take more adventurous visitors around the windswept Cape Horn. Ushuaia is also an important departure point for cruises to Antarctica.

Past and Present

"Their height appears greater than it really is, from their large guanaco mantles, their long flowing hair, and general figure... altogether they are certainly the tallest race we anywhere saw."

Charles Darwin, writing of the Tehuelches, native inhabitants of Patagonia

Argentina's history is very different from that of its Latin American neighbors to the north. The country had no ancient civilizations such as the Aztec and Maya of Mexico and Guatemala or the Inca of Peru. The native peoples, called Indians by the Spanish, were largely nomadic, and the Spanish conquest of their land that began in the early 16th century erased almost every trace of their culture. Only in the north was there an intermingling between native and Spanish cultures of the kind found, for example, in Mexico.

For some 300 years, Argentina was part of the vast Spanish colonies in the Americas. People thought of it as a remote, desolate place, and it attracted few settlers. Argentina's frontier status gave it a feel similar to North America's Wild West. Tough gauchos, or cowboys, herded cattle on the Pampas and clashed with the Indians. Only in Buenos Aires was there a large urban population.

In the early 19th century, Argentina freed itself from Spanish rule and began a long and often bloody struggle to form a nation. At the end of the 19th century, the country flourished: Immigration boosted the population and new territories were conquered. The road to nationhood, however, was hampered by tensions between Buenos Aires and the independent-minded provinces. Argentina's democracy has always been fragile, and the country has been vulnerable to the ambitions of dictators.

A spectacular reminder of Argentina's earliest peoples is the Cave of the Hands in Patagonia. Red, orange, and white painted hands smother the cave's walls.

FACT FILE

- The Spanish called the native peoples of America "Indians" because Christopher Columbus believed he had arrived in the Indies—that is, the islands of east Asia—and not a continent unknown to Europeans.
- Argentina became a fully independent nation on July 9, 1816. In Argentina, July 9 is celebrated with a public holiday, Independence Day.
- Argentina took its present name in 1860. After a war with Paraguay in 1874, it gained territory in the north. Patagonia became part of Argentina in 1881. By the late 19th century, its borders were much as they are today.

THE FIRST PEOPLES

The first inhabitants of the Americas entered the continent some 30,000 years ago, crossing the Bering Strait between present-day Alaska and Siberia. Gradually, they migrated throughout the continent, reaching Tierra del Fuego, at its southern tip, only in about 6,000 B.C. The migrating peoples adapted to the landscapes they found. Some settled in permanent villages and planted crops; others lived a nomadic (wandering) life of hunting and gathering.

Farmers and Nomads

Argentina and its neighbor Chile were the last parts of the American continent to be settled. The largest number of people lived in the northwestern highlands. Here peoples such as the Diaguita lived in simple stone houses in towns with populations as large as 3,000 people. About A.D. 650–850, many of these peoples fell under the influence of the Tiahuanaco empire of neighboring Bolivia and later of the Inca empire of Peru.

The first Europeans were struck by the strength and size of the Tehuelche people, or "Patagones," who wandered the steppes of present-day Patagonia.

To the east, in the rain forests of present-day Misiones, the Guaraní slashed and burned vegetation to make fields for growing sweet potatoes, corn, manioc, and beans. In the central mountains around present-day Córdoba, groups such as the Comechingones lived in villages and grew corn. Hunting rhea, deer, and wild pigs, and gathering plants, roots, and fruit, were important ways of getting food.

The remainder of the country to the south was only thinly populated. In this often harsh and inhospitable landscape, nomadic peoples survived by hunting and fishing. On the Pampas, the Querandí lived in *toldos*, tepees made from animal skins, and hunted rhea and guanaco (*see* p. 32) with bows and arrows or by throwing *bolas*. A *bola* was a set of three stones tied together with ropes. When thrown, the *bola* got tangled up in an animal's legs and made it fall.

In the far south, different peoples often specialized in certain kinds of food gathering or hunting. The Ona hunted the guanaco, while the Yagán ate fish, shellfish, and seals. While these hunter-gatherers have left behind no houses or monuments, archaeologists have discovered caves where these ancient peoples lived. The caves contain paintings dating back thousands of years that show scenes from daily life such as hunting guanacos.

Who Were Argentina's First Peoples?

Argentina's harsh terrain meant that most of the country's first peoples were nomadic hunters and gatherers. Only in the more fertile north were there permanent or semipermanent settlements, where peoples built houses and planted crops.

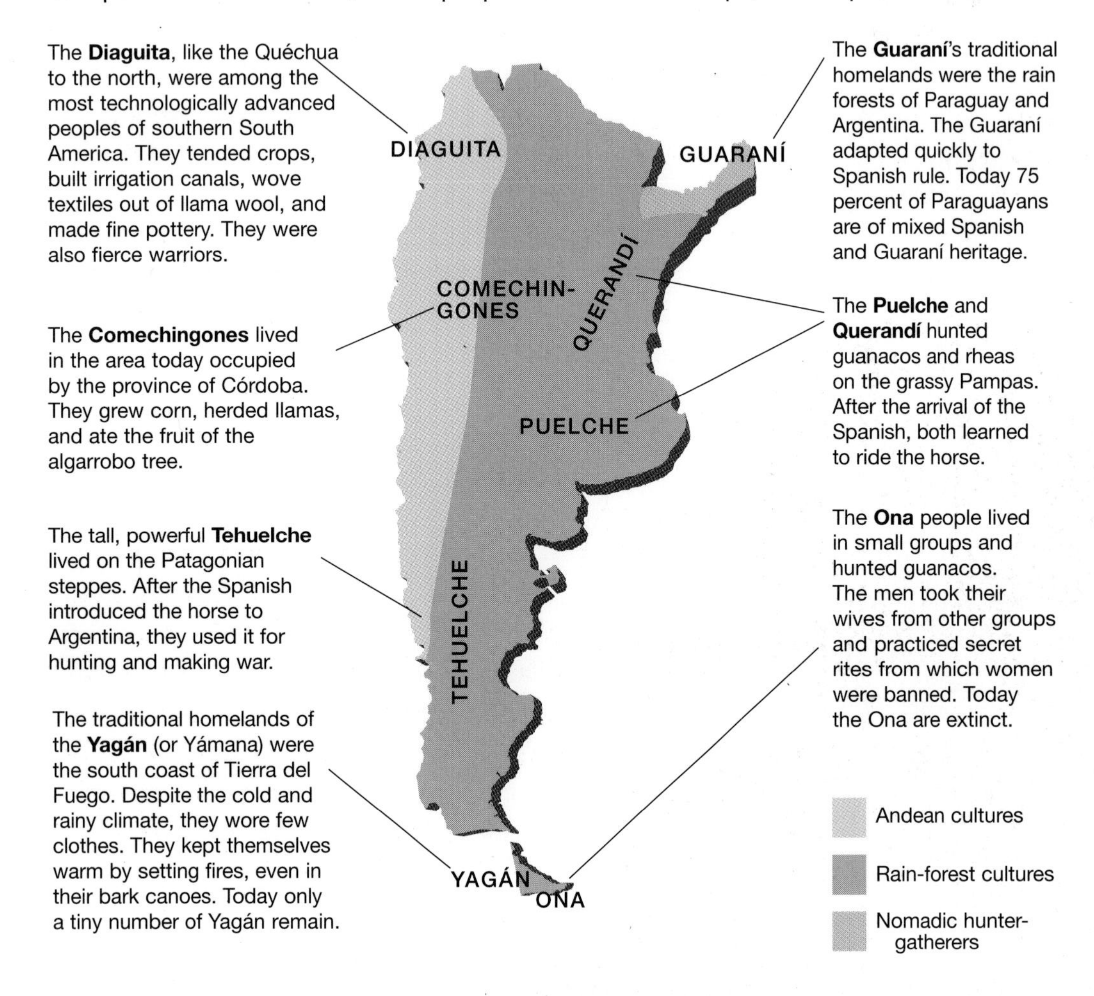

FIRST EXPEDITIONS TO SOUTHERN SOUTH AMERICA

In the 16th century, European explorers, including Ferdinand Magellan (pictured) began to explore the coasts and interior of Argentina.

THE SPANISH COLONY

After Christopher Columbus arrived in the Americas in 1492, a steady flow of explorers from Spain and Portugal crossed the Atlantic Ocean to explore the new continents. They came in search of the vast quantities of gold and silver supposed to be found there.

Explorers and Settlers

America was named in honor of the Italian explorer Amerigo Vespucci (1454–1512), who sailed down the eastern coast of South America with a Portuguese expedition in 1501–1502. The Argentines credit Juan Díaz de Solís (1470–1516), however, with being the first European to sail up the Río de la Plata, in 1516. He called this broad river estuary the Mar Dulce, the "Freshwater Sea," and hoped that it would provide a southwest passage to Asia. After he landed on one of its shores, he was killed and eaten by cannibal natives.

In 1520, a Spanish expedition under the leadership of Ferdinand Magellan successfully found the southwest passage by sailing through the treacherous straits that divide Tierra del Fuego from the South American mainland (*see* p. 54). In 1526, the Italian Sebastian Cabot (about 1476–1557) led yet another Spanish expedition to Argentina. He explored the Paraná and Paraguay rivers, and, in 1528, he founded the settlement of Sancto Spiritus ("Holy Spirit"). The Indians quickly overran the settlement and killed its inhabitants.

The Spanish were undeterred by such failures, however. The Portuguese were rapidly building an empire farther north in what later became Brazil, and the Spanish were eager not to be left behind. In 1535, the Spanish king sent another expedition to South America under the leadership of Pedro de Mendoza (1487–1537).

The Treaty of Tordesillas

After the arrival in America of Europeans in 1492, Spain and Portugal became rivals for territory in the New World. In 1493, the pope divided the non-Christian world between Spain and Portugal: All territories to the east of a north–south line in the Atlantic were to be Portuguese; all those to the west were to be Spanish. The following year, Spanish and Portuguese ambassadors met at Tordesillas in northwestern Spain and agreed to the pope's plan. On the basis of the Treaty of Tordesillas, the Spanish laid claim to the land that later became Argentina, while Brazil (then confined to the coast) became Portuguese.

The following year, Mendoza founded a settlement in what is today the *barrio* of La Boca (*see* p. 35–36), in Buenos Aires. He called the colony Puerto Nuestra Señora Santa María del Buen Aire, in thanksgiving for the "good wind" that had brought him to the country. After fierce Indian attacks, Mendoza was forced to abandon the settlement. He died on his way home to Spain.

Some of Mendoza's followers continued to explore farther up the Plata and Paraná rivers, sailing almost a thousand miles into the continent. In present-day

Explorers in South America brought back stories of the peoples and wildlife that they found there. In this drawing, an artist imagined the landscape around the Río de la Plata, filling it with fantastic creatures such as the "Indian raven" and the "iron pig."

Magellan in the Strait

The 350-mile (564 km) Strait of Magellan lies between the southern tip of South America and Tierra del Fuego and connects the Atlantic and Pacific oceans. The strait is named after the great Portuguese explorer Ferdinand Magellan (about 1480–1521), who led the first European expedition along this hazardous channel.

At the beginning of the 16th century, the Spanish were determined to find a sea route to the great western ocean known to exist on the other side of America. Magellan, who served the Spanish king, was entrusted with the task. In 1519, he set sail from the Spanish port of Sanlúcar de Barrameda with five ships and some 270 men. By December, he had reached the South American coast, and his ships made their way southward, keeping close to the shore.

Eventually, on October 21, 1520, the expedition rounded the coastline into a stormy, narrow strait. On either side of the strait loomed snowbound mountains. One of the ships, the *San Antonio,* deserted Magellan and headed back to Spain. Magellan and his remaining men, meanwhile, ventured farther along the strait. It took more than five weeks for them to reach the other end. The ships had to negotiate rip tides, fogs, and powerful winds. Finally, Magellan emerged into the calm ocean that lay on the other side. He gratefully called the ocean the Pacific—"the peaceful."

Paraguay, they found a fertile landscape inhabited by the friendly Guaraní Indians and founded Asunción—the first permanent Spanish settlement east of the Andes. Many settlers from Asuncíon later founded towns in northern Argentina, including Córdoba and Salta. Spaniards from Chile founded the towns of Mendoza, San Juan, and San Luis.

Building Towns

The Spanish kings strictly regulated the planning of new towns in their colonies. Settlements had to be built on a grid plan based on a central plaza whose four corners faced the compass points. One rule ran as follows: "When the new town is being built, the settlers...shall try to avoid communication with the Indians...Nor are the Indians to enter the settlement until it is complete...so that when the Indians see [it] they will be filled with wonder and will realize that the Spaniards are settling there permanently."

Viceroyalties and *Audiencias*

The Spanish developed a complicated structure in order to rule their massive American empire. The Spanish New World colonies were divided into two viceroyalties, each governed by a viceroy, or governor. The Spanish territories to the north of the Isthmus of Panama became the Viceroyalty of New Spain, governed from Mexico City. Those to the south largely fell within the Viceroyalty of Peru and were governed from Lima. The viceroys ruled in the name of the Spanish king, who never visited America.

Because the viceroyalties were so vast, each was divided into a number of realms, or "kingdoms," administered by a body called an *audiencia*. In the 16th century, for example, six *audiencias* were established within the Viceroyalty of Peru. What is today Argentina fell under the jurisdiction of the *audiencia* of Charcas.

There was a rigid social structure. In each viceroyalty, the viceroy and the other high officials usually came from Spain—the *peninsulares*. Next came the *criollos*, people of European origin who were born in the Spanish colonies. Next were the *mestizos*—people of mixed Spanish and Indian blood. At the bottom of the social scale were the Indians whom the Spanish had conquered.

The Indians were treated like slaves and were often moved from where they lived to be sent to work in mines in the Andes or on lands far from their homes.

Lima, the capital of the Viceroyalty of Peru, was originally called the "City of the Kings." This was because it was founded on January 6—the Feast of the Three Kings.

The capital of Charcas was La Paz, today the capital of Bolivia.

Jesuit Missions

The Society of Jesus, or Jesuit Order, was a religious movement founded in 1534 by the Spanish Catholic reformer Ignatius of Loyola. An important aim of the order was to convert non-Christians to Christianity. Members of the order were priests known as Jesuits.

The Jesuits first arrived in South America in 1549. From 1608, the Jesuits began to organize self-sufficient communities for converted Guaraní Indians. Most of the communities, called missions, were located in an area that today straddles eastern Paraguay and the far northeast of Argentina.

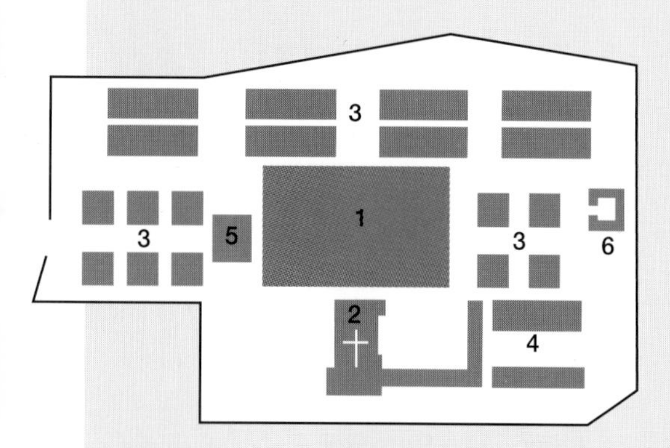

1 Plaza (square) 2 Cathedral 3 Indian quarters 4 Workshops 5 Town hall 6 Jail

The missions were based on a grid system (shown above), with a central square from which all the streets extended at right angles. The plaza was usually enclosed with religious buildings. The Indians were housed in communal huts.

The Indians' main work was farming crops and tending the mission's livestock. Life for the Indians was generally better than under the *encomiendas* (*see* p. 57). Many Indians chose to work at a mission rather than for other Spaniards.

The success of the missions attracted unwelcome attention. Portuguese slave raiders from São Paulo in Brazil destroyed many of the settlements and abducted the Indians. Native chieftains also led attacks on the missions. Disease, too, took its toll. The Indians lacked immunity to European diseases such as smallpox, and many died.

Eventually these problems, together with general suspicion of their activities, led to the Jesuits being expelled from South America in 1767. The missions gradually fell into ruin, and many were overgrown by the jungle. Today some of the missions have been opened to the public. The picture above shows an overhead shot of the ruins of the cathedral at San Ignacio Miní, close to Posadas in Misiones.

When European settlers were given land, they were often also given Indians to work the land. This system was called *encomienda*. The Europeans were supposed to convert the Indians to Christianity but were more interested in getting the Indians to do as much work as possible.

Many Indians did not have enough to eat and worked so hard that they were vulnerable to the new diseases that the Europeans brought with them. Thousands died from diseases such as influenza and measles. As fewer Indians

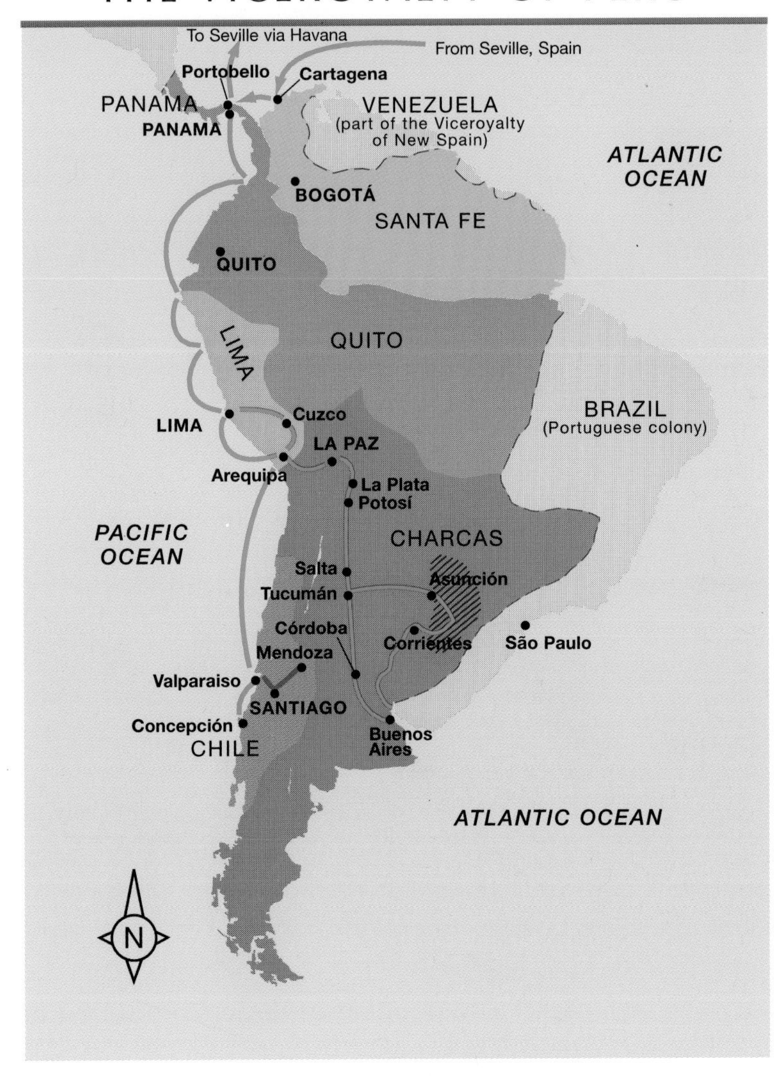

In the mid-17th century, South America was divided between the Spanish and Portuguese empires. Spanish South America was known as the Viceroyalty of Peru and comprised six smaller* audiencias. *Trade to and from Peru was handled by two ports in the far north of South America—Cartagena and Portobello. Buenos Aires lay at the very end of the inland trading routes.

Area of Jesuit missions

became available to work the land, the *criollos* replaced the *encomiendas* with large landholdings, where they grew crops and grazed livestock. The *mestizos* and Indians had to make do with small plots of inferior land or to work on the large estates. The *criollo* landholdings became the *estancias*—or ranches—that formed the backbone of the Argentine economy.

During the 17th and 18th centuries, the Spanish kings kept tight control of the South American trade routes. They banned the export and import of goods along the Río de la Plata. Instead, minerals from the Andean mines, for example, had to be transported a long way north to Panama. From there, they were sent by ship to Spain.

Buenos Aires and the surrounding region remained unimportant economically. The town had to earn a living by smuggling in European goods from Portuguese-controlled Brazil. These contraband goods were half or a third the price of the official imports. By contrast, some towns, such as Córdoba, flourished during this period thanks to the northern trade routes.

The "Lost People"

From its earliest days, some inhabitants of Buenos Aires fled the city for the freedom of the Pampas. Some were criminals escaping the law; others were soldiers deserting the army or escaped slaves. They were known as *la gente perdida,* "the lost people." On the Pampas, they had a harsh lifestyle, slaughtering cattle for their meat and hides. They wore baggy trousers and shawls and carried a special knife called a *facón*. The women, or *chinas,* brought up the children in simple houses that were very like the Indians'. The lifestyle of the "lost people" helped shape that of the gaucho.

The Rise of Buenos Aires

In the mid-18th century, Argentina's seat of power began to shift from the northwest region to Buenos Aires. As less gold, silver, and other metals were coming from the Andean mines, the Spanish king realized that it would be better to encourage trade in his South American colonies and have a direct shipping route from an Atlantic port on the South American continent. In 1776, a new viceroyalty, Río de la Plata, was created with its capital at Buenos Aires. The effect on the city was dramatic. The population grew from 2,200 in 1726 to more than 33,000 in little more than 50 years.

INDEPENDENCE

In 1806, a small British force under Sir Home Popham invaded Buenos Aires. The British were building a powerful sea empire and wanted to gain control of the profitable trading routes between Europe and the Río de la Plata. When the Spanish viceroy fled, a British victory seemed certain. Popham had not reckoned on local resistance, however, and his men were pushed back by a force of Spanish and local soldiers.

The British made another attempt the next year with 6,000 soldiers. The city's inhabitants fired on the invading troops from the rooftops, using cannon and musketry captured during the first British invasion. So many of the British soldiers were either injured or killed in the invasion that the British soon retreated.

Argentines recall their struggle for independence with two national holidays—Revolution of 1810 Day (May 25) and Independence Day (July 9).

Belgrano and the Junta

The Spanish soldiers stationed in the viceroyalty did little to defend the territory from the British. Local-born *criollos*, people of Spanish

This statue in front of the Casa Rosada in Buenos Aires's Plaza de Mayo commemorates the Argentine hero Manuel Belgrano, who helped lead his country to independence.

descent born in Argentina, realized they could expect little help from their Spanish rulers. They began to believe they would be far better off if they were independent of the Spanish Crown.

In the early 19th century, many parts of South America declared independence. This map shows the independence dates. Some of the new nations proved short-lived; others, such as Argentina, later changed their name.

Events in Europe pushed the *criollo* dream of independence nearer to reality. In 1808, the French emperor Napoleon Bonaparte (1769–1821) invaded Spain. On May 25, 1810, the people of Buenos Aires took their chance and deposed the Spanish viceroy. In his place, they set up a revolutionary *junta*, a small ruling committee of the military men who had led the coup against the Spanish. Nevertheless, the junta still continued to rule in the name of the Spanish king Ferdinand VII. Argentines often date their independence from the date of the coup—May 25, 1810.

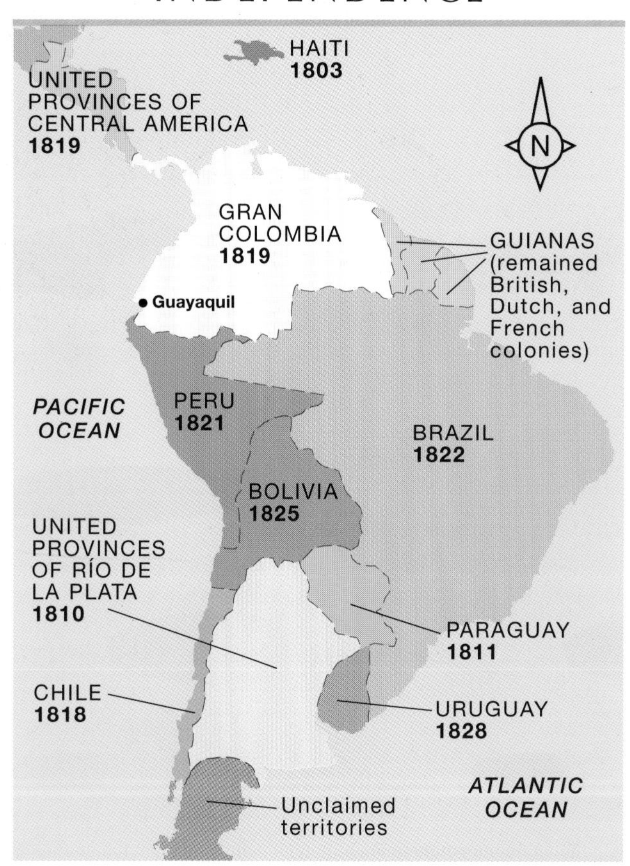

The junta included Manuel Belgrano (1770–1820), who was the son of a wealthy Buenos Aires family. Belgrano had studied in Spain and had returned to Argentina full of the revolutionary ideas popular in Europe at the time, including the right of a people to govern themselves.

Belgrano and others who shared his ideas could not convince the most powerful social class, comprising of rich merchants, *estancieros* (ranchers), and the Roman Catholic church, that it was important to reform the country. Because this ruling group rejected change, it was difficult for all Argentines to unite behind the independence movement. Two opposing groups emerged. One, the *Unitarios* (Unitarians), wanted a centralized government that operated from Buenos Aires, while the *Federales* (Federalists) preferred to have self-governing provinces within a federal system.

For six years, the two groups fought over how the country should be governed. When soldiers from the Viceroyalty of Peru threatened to invade Buenos Aires in July 1816, the provinces united together under the blue and white banner of Belgrano to stop an enemy invasion. On July 9, 1816, the Argentines declared their independence at the Congress of Tucumán—six years after the original declaration of independence. They called their new country the United Provinces of Río de la Plata.

Even today, Argentines honor José de San Martín as their greatest hero. Here San Martín is shown crossing the Andes in a dashing style that recalls paintings of Napoleon crossing the Alps.

José de San Martín

Declaring independence was one thing; making Spanish troops leave South America was another. The man who succeeded in doing this was José de San Martín (1778–1850).

San Martín enjoys a reputation as one of the liberators of Spanish-speaking South America. He fought in the south of the continent, while Simon Bolívar, another great name in the fight for independence, battled farther north. San Martín agreed with Belgrano that it would be better for Argentina to stay a monarchy, and he shared hopes with Bolívar of uniting all of Spanish America after independence. He failed in both things, but his military achievements won him a special place in Argentine history.

Like Manuel Belgrano, José San Martín was born into a wealthy *criollo* family and was educated in Spain. He served as an officer in the Spanish army in Spain,

although his true desire was for Latin American independence. In 1812, San Martín returned to Argentina and took charge of an army of liberation.

After preparing his army for two years, San Martín led 3,778 men across the Andes Mountains into Chile in 1817. There he secured the country's independence before launching an attack on Lima, the center of Spanish power in South America. In July 1821, he assumed control of the new republic of Peru. His position, however, was far from secure.

After the Viceroyalty of Río de la Plata won its independence in 1816, the city of Buenos Aires flourished. Cafés opened and horses-and-buggies raced through the streets. In aristocratic houses, couples danced the minuet. In 1821, Buenos Aires also became the home of South America's first university.

In 1822, San Martín met with Simon Bolívar, now president of the independent republic of Gran Colombia, at Guayaquil in what is today Ecuador. What exactly happened during their secret discussions, no one quite knows. All that is certain is that San Martín suddenly resigned his position in Lima and left South America for Europe. Lonely and disillusioned, he died in France in 1850. It was left to Bolívar to complete the liberation of South America. In 1880, San Martín's body was ceremoniously returned to Buenos Aires and placed in the cathedral.

For Argentines, San Martín is a hero and a symbol of sacrifice, bravery, and lack of self-interest. He is called the "*Héroe de la Patria*" ("Hero of the Nation"). Many statues of San Martín were put up, and many towns have a street or square named in his honor.

DICTATORS AND DEMOCRATS

The next 50 years of Argentine history were marked by fighting between the Federalists and the Unitarians. The Federalists were mainly rich landowners, who under Spanish rule had enjoyed a large degree of independence and power in the regions. As Buenos Aires grew in importance, the Federalists grew increasingly resentful. In 1835, the ambitious Federalist Juan Manuel de Rosas (1793–1877) seized power in Buenos Aires and became *caudillo* (*see* box) of the surrounding province.

The Red and the Blue

Rosas was born in Buenos Aires in 1793. He was brought up, however, on his family's *estancia*, where he came to admire the gauchos. Between 1829 and 1832, Rosas was governor of Buenos Aires. After his term of office had finished, Rosas led a brutal military campaign against the Indians of the south. In what became known as the Desert Campaign of 1833–1834, his troops massacred thousands of Indians.

Away from the battlefields, in Buenos Aires, Rosas's wife campaigned to have her husband reappointed governor of Buenos Aires. She formed a mass-movement, called the *Sociedad Popular Restauradora* ("Society for Popular Restoration"), which appealed to all social classes. The movement had an armed wing called La Mazorca because its symbol was an ear of wheat (*mazorca* in Spanish). La Mazorca terrorized Argentine society for the next 20 years, torturing and executing its opponents. Even the Roman Catholic church rallied to Rosas's cause, allowing his portrait to be displayed in churches.

The Caudillos

After independence, ambitious local leaders called *caudillos* emerged throughout South America. *Caudillos* built up considerable military and political power and were able to claim significant positions in government. The *caudillo* José Antonio Páez, for example, became president of Venezuela. *Caudillos* often claimed to be upholders of the law—Rosas (below), for example, was known as the "Restorer of the Laws." They often resorted to violence, however. Domingo Faustimo Sarmiento, who later became president, said of Rosas: "[He] applied the knife of the gaucho to the culture of Buenos Aires and undid the work of centuries—of civilization, law, and liberty."

Darwin in South America

Charles Robert Darwin (1809–1882) was a British naturalist best known for his theories of evolution. He was born in Shrewsbury, England, and studied at the universities of Edinburgh and Cambridge. In Darwin's final year at Cambridge, a professor recommended him for an unpaid post as the official naturalist aboard HMS *Beagle*, which was commissioned to chart the coasts of South America.

In 1831, the *Beagle* set sail under Captain Robert Fitzroy (1805–1865). At that time, Darwin was a directionless young graduate. The five-year voyage gave him a chance to think, study, and gain confidence in his skills as a scientist. He collected wildlife and fossils and made clear notes on both. Contrary to popular myth, he did not experience a revelation on evolutionary theory while on the voyage. Instead, he built up a store of knowledge that he would later rely on in his researches.

Darwin is usually associated with the study of biology. However, during the voyage he spent more time studying geology. He became a follower of the controversial theories of Charles Lyell (1797–1875). Lyell rejected the biblical account of creation and argued that the landscape was shaped by natural processes that took place over millions of years.

Lyell's theories encouraged Darwin to look at the biological world in a similar way. In his book *On the Origin of Species*, published years later in 1859, he contradicted the Bible's explanation for the variety in living things with his theory that natural processes were responsible for biology as well as geology.

Opposite: ***A contemporary watercolor shows HMS*** **Beagle** ***in the Murray Narrow, off Tierra del Fuego.***

He called this theory "natural selection." Many people, including the *Beagle*'s former captain, Robert Fitzroy, condemned the book as heretical—that is, contrary to accepted religious truths.

During the *Beagle*'s voyage, however, Captain Fitzroy encouraged Darwin's researches agreeing to allow Darwin to leave the ship for lengthy periods to explore the land. South America filled Darwin with wonder and awe, and during his explorations, he enjoyed many adventures.

In the Pampas, he set off with gauchos (*see* p. 21) on horseback, and, in Patagonia, he hunted rheas. He suffered mountain sickness crossing the Andes and nearly got stranded while exploring the land among the channels of Tierra del Fuego. In the Falklands/Malvinas, he puzzled over the origins of the islands' only land mammal, the foxlike *warrah* (now extinct). In the Galápagos Islands, off Ecuador, he rode a giant tortoise and "found it a very wobbly seat."

On his return to England in 1836, Darwin quickly found his place in London's scientific community. He was able to publish his observations in journals and books, such as *The Voyage of the Beagle* (1839). In private, he began work on his theory of evolution.

The *Beagle*'s voyage around the Argentine coastline is remembered in many of the country's place-names, such as the Beagle Channel in Tierra del Fuego and the Fitzroy Mountains in Patagonia, named for the ship's captain.

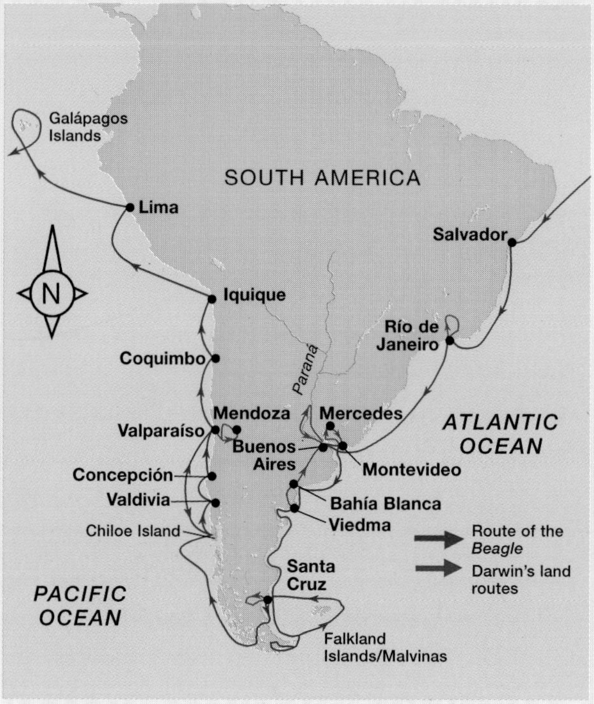

Left: ***While the*** **Beagle** ***charted the South American coastline, Darwin explored inland. The young scientist visited some of Argentina's growing towns and cities as well as roaming its vast wildernesses.***

After his return from the Desert Campaign in April 1835, Rosas once again became governor of Buenos Aires and extended his power throughout the United Provinces by crushing other *caudillos*. One of his first decrees was that everyone had to wear red, which was the Federalist color. Women wore scarlet dresses, and men red badges with the slogan "Federation or Death." Wearing blue—the Unitarian color—meant risking being sent to prison or being executed.

Under Rosas's reign of terror, people lived in fear for more than 20 years. In 1852, revolutionaries, supported by the governments of Uruguay and Brazil, overthrew Rosas. The ex-dictator fled to England, where he lived until his death in 1877.

The Conquest of the Wilderness

Throughout the 18th and 19th centuries, European settlers met resistance from the Indians whose lands they were taking away. In one attack close to Buenos Aires in 1876, Indians reportedly captured 500 settlers and 500,000 head of cattle. In 1879, General Julio Roca led an army south against the Indians to seize the remaining lands that were still in native hands. All the land was sold in advance to pay for the campaign. Soldiers from Buenos Aires, Córdoba, San Luis, and Mendoza joined up at the Negro River and marched into Patagonia. There they conquered or exterminated the nomadic Tehuelche people. The expedition became known as the *Conquista del desierto* ("conquest of the wilderness"). Those Indians who survived were put into reservations.

Building a Modern State

Once Rosas was removed from power, people wanted stability. Justo José de Urquiza (1801–1870), who had led the resistance to Rosas, helped draw up a constitution. The Argentine constitution, based on that of the United States, was formally adopted on May 1, 1853. At the time, the constitution was unique in South America. It contained a bill of rights, abolished slavery, and set up independent courts. Urquiza became one of the first presidents under the new constitution. He oversaw the building of schools, established a national bank, and built better transportation links.

Urquiza's work was continued by a succession of reforming presidents, including Bartolomé Mitre and Domingo Faustimo Sarmiento. Sarmiento, for example, was committed to popular education, setting up the first teacher-training college as well as bringing teachers from the United States.

GROWTH OF ARGENTINA

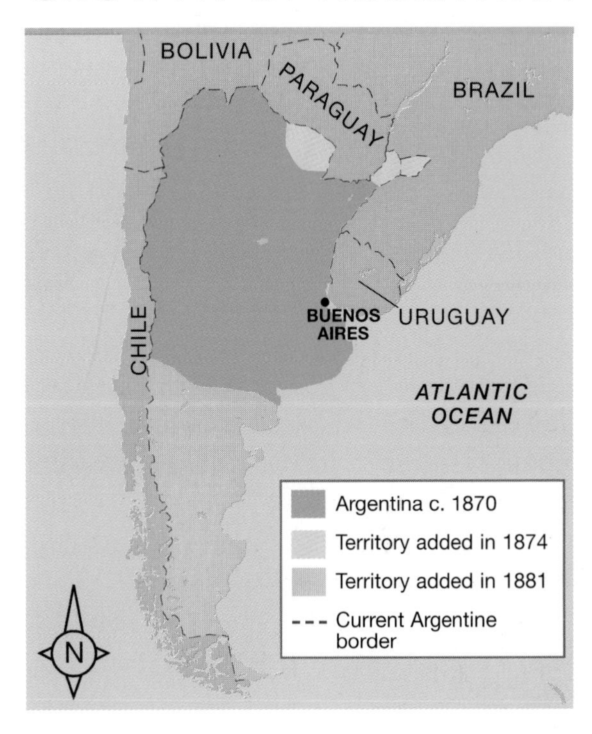

By the 1880s, the map of Argentina looked much as it does today. Argentina's triumph in the Paraguayan War added new territories in the north, while campaigns in the south laid claim to Patagonia.

Foreign investors built railroads that linked Buenos Aires with outlying provinces. By 1862, Buenos Aires had won acceptance as the capital of a united Argentina, although it was not formally recognized as such until 1880.

During the 1870s, Argentina also won vast new territories. In the Paraguayan War (1865–1870), an alliance of Argentina, Brazil, and Uruguay defeated the Paraguayan dictator Francisco Solano López (1827–1870). Victory brought Argentina Paraguayan territories that later became the Argentine provinces of Formosa, Chaco, and Misiones. Territory was also seized in the south, where General Julio Roca led another campaign against the Indians of the Pampas (*see* box opposite).

The Golden Age

Between 1880 and the start of World War I in 1914, Argentina prospered. It changed from a rural, backward country into a thriving urban-based nation. Every year, thousands of immigrants arrived in Buenos Aires to work in the factories or on the *estancias*. Foreign countries, especially Great Britain, found Argentina's booming economy attractive and made large investments.

The new wealth encouraged the growth of a powerful middle class, who supported new newspapers and founded new political parties, such as the *Unión Cívica Radical*, the Radical Party. Intellectual life flourished, and the Teatro Colón (*see* p. 40) opened in Buenos Aires.

Between 1870 and 1920, some 3.5 million immigrants arrived in Argentina.

In 1914, World War I broke out in Europe. Argentina took no part in the war. At first, though, the country benefited from the war economically. Argentina exported large quantities of canned and frozen meat to Europe to feed the soldiers fighting on both sides. As the war developed, however, Argentina experienced difficulties as food prices rose and wages fell. Many working people lost their jobs or had to work much longer hours.

The people of Buenos Aires grew restless. Thousands joined unions and demanded more rights. There were strikes on the docks and the railroads. The government reacted by firing workers. In 1919, in what is known as *Semana Trágica* ("Tragic Week"), soldiers opened fire on strikers and killed many of them.

The Great Depression, which began in the United States in 1929, added to Argentina's difficulties as the world economy slumped. The country's weak government lurched from crisis to crisis, and the discontented army increasingly acted as an independent political force. In 1930, a military coup, or takeover, seized power from the Radical Party government. Although the radicals regained power in 1937, they were not effective rulers.

When World War II broke out in 1939, Argentina once again was neutral. There was more popular unrest, however, and, in 1943, the government was overthrown by another military coup.

Immigrants arrive in Buenos Aires in the late 19th century. As Argentina grew more prosperous, thousands of people from Spain and Italy poured into the country to work on the docks and in the meat-packing plants of the capital or to help build railroads.

Argentine president Juan Perón and his wife Eva ("Evita") enjoyed widespread support in Argentina, particularly among working people. Even today, people debate whether Juan Perón was an inspirational president or a ruthless dictator. Here the couple ride through Buenos Aires in an open-top automobile.

THE RULE OF PERÓN

One of the leaders of the coup was an unknown army colonel, Juan Domingo Perón (1895–1974). Juan Perón was born in Buenos Aires province in 1895. At age 16, he joined the Argentine army and rose to the rank of colonel. Being in the army gave Perón the opportunity to travel throughout Argentina and overseas. He saw that although his country was growing richer, the people who benefited most from the prosperity were the landowners.

During the 1930s, Perón served as a military aide in Italy. There he was deeply impressed by the fascist dictator Benito Mussolini. Like Mussolini, Perón wanted his country to be strong and powerful and was prepared to use violence to achieve his goals.

Perón for President

When a group of army officers overthrew President Ramón S. Castillo on June 4, 1943, Perón became secretary of the labor and social welfare ministry. His labor reforms made him extremely popular among working people, some of whom achieved job security and pensions for the first time. Perón also set up his own private army.

Members of Perón's army were nicknamed the *descamisados* ("the shirtless") because many of them were poor workers.

The other military leaders were alarmed by Perón's popularity and put him in prison. Rallied by Perón's fiancée, Eva Duarte (*see* box opposite), thousands of *descamisados* ("the shirtless") and others took part in public demonstrations. Within weeks, Perón was freed. He made a triumphant speech from the balcony of the Casa Rosada to the 30,000 people gathered in the Plaza de Mayo below. In 1946, the discredited generals held elections for president, which Perón won with 54 percent of the vote.

During the late 1940s, Argentina's economy flourished. New industries were set up and wages increased. All the while, however, Péron took away people's rights. Opposition newspapers were closed down, teachers and civil servants were forced to join Péron's party if they wanted to keep their jobs, and opponents were persecuted and sometimes tortured and killed. Péron also rewrote the constitution, allowing the president to seek re-election for an unlimited number of six-year terms.

Both prosperity and repression helped Perón gain a second term as president in 1951, this time with a 67 percent majority. There were problems just over the horizon, however. Drought and falling grain prices affected the economy badly, and, in 1952, Eva Perón died, causing a national outburst of grief. The political tide now turned against Perón. In 1955, rich landowners, the Roman Catholic church, and the military combined to overthrow the president and send him into exile. Perón eventually settled in Madrid in Spain.

Justicialisimo

Perón called his ideas about social justice and national unity *justicialismo*, or "Justicialism," and enshrined them in a new constitution in 1949. *Justicialismo* meant strong government with rights over private property, land, and national resources. Accordingly, under Perón's rule, the banks, railroads, and docks were brought under national control. *Justicialismo* formed the basis for the political ideology later known as Peronism.

Perón Returns to Power

Perón remained in exile for 18 years. During this time, Argentina had nine successive leaders. The military leaders were determined to keep supporters of Perón and his ideas out of Argentina. They repeatedly overthrew elected presidents and replaced them with generals. Perón, meanwhile, kept a watchful eye on his country's progress. When his supporter Héctor Cámpora won just under half the votes in the presidential election of 1973, Perón returned to Argentina. Some 500,000 people came to Buenos Aires airport to greet him. Fighting between Perón's supporters and the police left hundreds of people dead or wounded. Then Cámpora resigned, and a new election was held in September, which Perón won with 62 percent of the vote. Barely a year into his third term as president, Perón died suddenly, on July 1, 1974.

As president, Perón was called *"El Conductor"*—"the leader"—echoing the name given to the Italian dictator Mussolini—*"il Duce."*

Although Perón ruled his country for a total of only 11 years, his ideas are still powerful today and are known as *peronismo* (Peronism). Argentines either love or hate Perón. His supporters say that he improved workers' living conditions. His opponents consider Perón a dictator.

Evita

Born into a poor family in 1919, María Eva Duarte left home for Buenos Aires at the age of 15 determined to become an actress. Six years later, she had her own radio show. Contacts introduced her to many leading army officers, among them Juan Perón. When they married in October 1945, he was 49 and she was 25.

Eva Perón used her position to improve the position of women and the poor. She set up the Eva Perón Foundation, which provided free health care and education for the poor. Her energy and glamor won her huge popularity among Argentina's workers, who called her *"la Madonna de América"* ("the Madonna of America"). People felt they knew her so well, they even called her "Evita"—the affectionate form of Eva.

Diagnosed with cancer in 1951, Evita died on July 26, 1952, aged only 33. Her tomb in the Recoleta Cemetery (*see* p. 41) in Buenos Aires bears the inscription, "Don't cry for me, Argentina, I am near you."

FROM DICTATORSHIP TO DEMOCRACY

After Perón's death, his third wife, Isabel, took power, She was no Evita, however, and was soon removed from power in another army coup on March 24, 1976. The next 15 years of Argentine history were the darkest since the Rosas dictatorship. The military government dissolved the congress, outlawed all political parties, and placed the universities and trade unions under the army's control.

To this day, the Mothers of the Plaza de Mayo protest every Thursday in Buenos Aires's main square—the Plaza de Mayo. They demand information about their "disappeared" children, murdered under the military dictatorship.

The Dirty War

In 1976, the "Dirty War" began. Since 1969, guerrilla groups such as the Peronist *Montoneros* and the Marxist *Ejército Revolucionario del Pueblo* (People's Revolutionary Army) had been kidnapping people and robbing banks. They wanted to raise funds and draw attention to their causes in the newspapers. After 1976, however, the army began ruthlessly exterminating the guerrilla groups.

The army arrested anyone whom they suspected of being sympathetic to the guerrillas or of disagreeing with the government. The presence of a green Ford Falcon automobile, without license plates and occupied by men wearing sunglasses, terrified Argentina's civilians. Once taken away, there was little hope that an individual would come back.

Human-rights campaigners estimate that during the Dirty War, between 1976 and 1983, some 15,000 people "disappeared." These people, who became known as *los desaparecidos* ("the ones who disappeared"), were kidnapped, tortured, raped, and murdered by soldiers, police, and right-wing death squads. Some 300 children also disappeared. Some *desaparecidos* were drugged and thrown still alive from military planes into the Río de la Plata at night. The Dirty War stopped only when the military had another war to fight.

The South Atlantic War

Many Argentines had long resented what they saw as the British occupation of the Islas Malvinas/Falkland Islands (*see* p. 28). On April 2, 1982, the military leader and president General Leopoldo Galtieri ordered the invasion of the islands. He hoped that a swift victory would revive support for his military regime. A small Argentine force of 5,000 men quickly captured the British garrison, and appointed an Argentine military governor.

To Galtieri's surprise, the British sent a naval force to recapture the islands. In the war that followed, 746 Argentines and 256 British soldiers died before the Argentines surrendered on June 14, 1982. The Argentines' inglorious defeat, combined with rocketing inflation at home, brought an end to the rule of General Galtieri and the army.

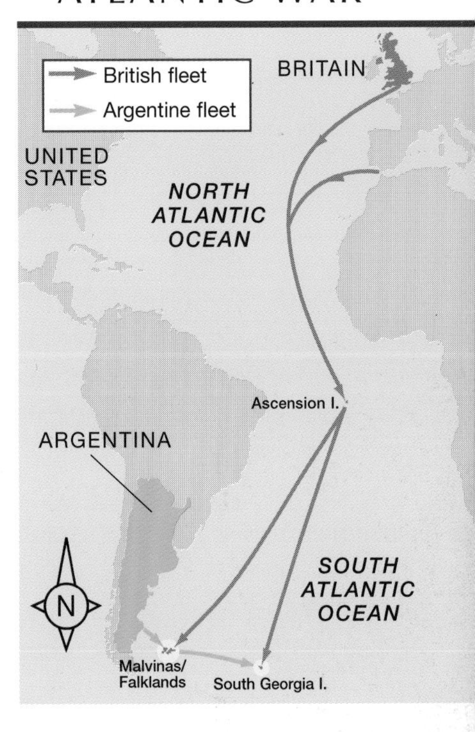

The Argentine army invaded the Malvinas/Falklands on April 2, 1982, and South Georgia Island on the following day. The British Task Force sailed some 8,000 miles (13,000 km) to retake the islands.

The Return to Democracy

In September 1983, elections were held in Argentina. Raúl Alfonsín of the Radical Party was elected president. A report into those who "disappeared," *Nunca más* ("Never Again"), was published in 1984. It forced Argentines to accept as true all the stories they had hoped were exaggerated and led to public demands for those responsible to be brought to trial. Some officers were found guilty, but President Alfonsín agreed with the military not to prosecute more officers because so many had been involved. Protests from the public over this helped to end his presidency.

A guard keeps watch at the Buenos Aires memorial to the Argentine soldiers who died during the South Atlantic War.

In 1989, Carlos Menem, governor of La Rioja province, became president. As leader of the Peronist Party, Menem campaigned with promises of higher wages that appealed to the workers. After his election, however, he carried out drastic measures to reform the economy. He embraced free enterprise and sold off many of Argentina's national companies, such as the airline *Aerolíneas Argentinas*. Although he succeeded in bringing inflation under control, unemployment was on the rise.

Increasingly, President Carlos Menem made many new laws without consulting Congress (such laws are called decrees) or vetoed laws that had been passed by Congress. Many people accused Menem of ruling undemocratically and were angry that he pardoned all the military for their crimes. After serving two terms in office, Menem was replaced by Fernando de la Rúa in 1999.

President Menem's authoritarian style, his strict economic reforms, and his release of the generals responsible for the "Dirty War" made him a controversial figure.

THE ARGENTINE ADMINISTRATION

Like the United States, Argentina is a federal republic. It is made up of 23 provinces and one federal district (Buenos Aires). For much of Argentina's history as an independent nation, there was a struggle between the supporters of a strong central government, based in Buenos Aires, and the supporters of provincial governments. A compromise was reached in 1853, when a constitution was agreed on that was based on the federal model of the United States. With some amendments, this remains the one in place today.

The Argentine system of government is modeled on that of the United States.

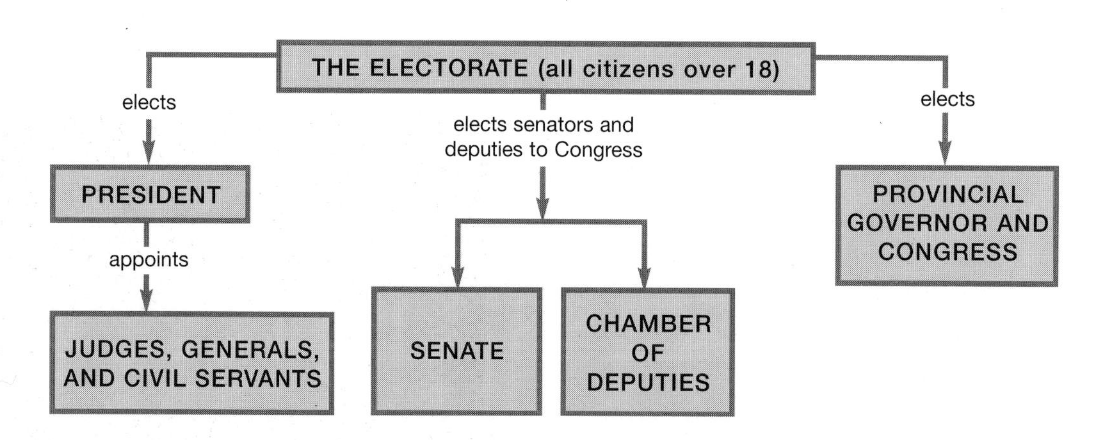

THE NATIONAL CONGRESS IN 2000

President: Fernando de la Rúa • President is elected by popular vote for a 4-year term

Senate
72 members • From 2001, elections to be held every 2 years

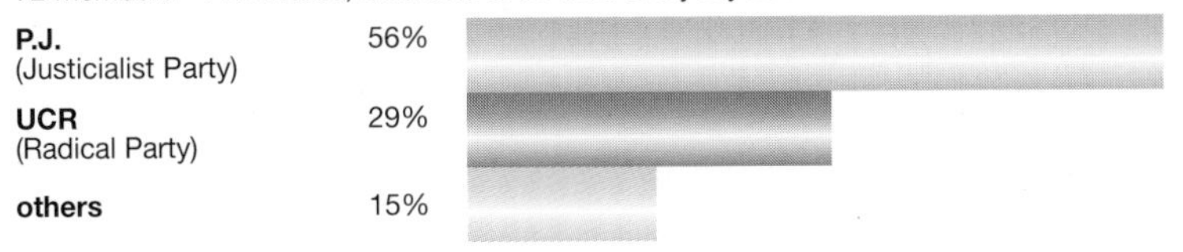

Chamber of Deputies
257 members • Last election 1999 • Half of members elected every 2 years for a 4-year term

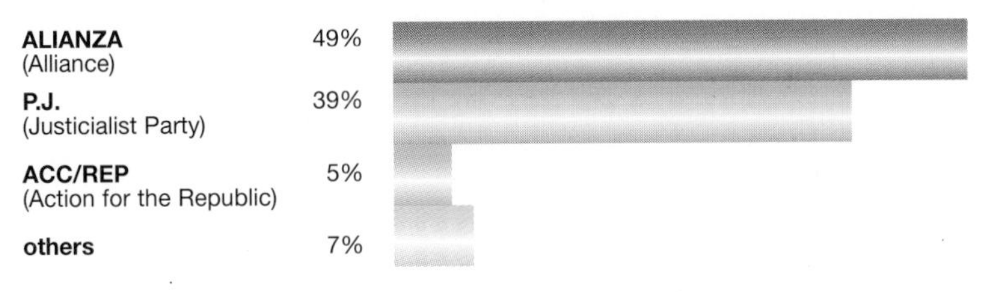

The most important political parties are the Justicialist Party, which draws together Peronist groups, and the Radical Party, led by Fernando de la Rúa. The Alianza is an alliance of centrist parties that includes the Radical Party.

Executive power—the power to enforce the law—rests finally with the president. The president is elected along with a vice-president every four years and, following an amendment of 1994, can now serve up to two terms of four years. The president and vice-president must follow the Roman Catholic religion. The president is the supreme commander of the armed forces and appoints the nation's judges, generals, and senior civil servants.

The National Congress (*Congreso Nacional*) holds legislative power—that is, it has the power to make laws. The Congress consists of two houses: a Senate and a Chamber of Deputies. The Senate used to be made up of appointed representatives from the provinces. From 2001, however, it will be a fully elected chamber, with 72 members. The 257-member Chamber of Deputies is elected under a system of proportional representation and sits for a term of four years. The two houses debate, alter, and finally pass or reject laws that are set before them. Each of the provinces has its own elected Congress and governor. who has considerable local power.

The National Congress stands at the western end of the broad Avenida de Mayo in Buenos Aires. At the eastern end is the Plaza de Mayo, where the presidential palace, the Casa Rosada stands.

The Economy

"As rich as an Argentine."

French saying

Traditionally, the basis of Argentina's economy was agriculture and, in particular, cattle raising. The danger with relying on one industry is that a country's wealth depends on world prices that can change dramatically from year to year. As a result, Argentina's prosperity has always been unstable. A century ago, the economy was booming and attracting European immigrants with the promise of jobs. Argentina was considered a wealthy country with good prospects. In France, the saying "as rich as an Argentine" could often be heard.

Today Argentina's economy is not as healthy as it was in the late 19th century. Despite having a well-educated workforce and a wealth of natural resources such as fertile farmland and oil, Argentina has failed to fulfill its economic potential. Argentina's economic difficulties are often blamed on the country's agitated political history, which has slowed economic growth.

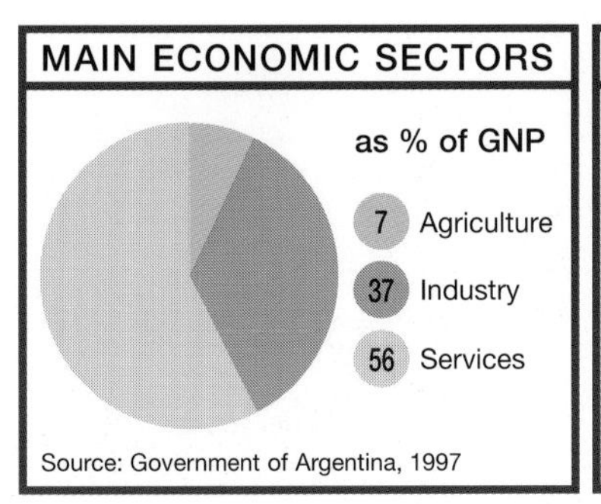

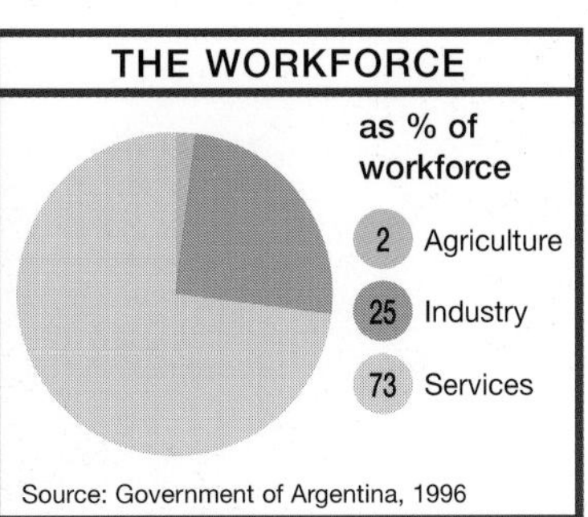

Cattle raising remains an important industry in Argentina. On ranches, cattle are herded into pens so that they can be examined and marked.

FACT FILE

- At more than $6,000, Argentina's annual income per person is the highest in Latin America.
- At $295 billion, Argentina's gross national product (GNP) is the third largest in Latin America.
- Argentina has often suffered from high inflation. During the rule of President Isabel Perón, it stood at over 500 percent. In 1997, however, it was just 0.5 percent.
- Argentina is a member of MERCOSUR—a South American trading bloc that includes Brazil, Uruguay, and Paraguay.

MAJOR SECTORS

Argentina's most important resource remains its land and, in particular, the vast fertile Pampas that stretch south and west of the capital, Buenos Aires. In the 20th century, however, other economic sectors such as industry and services have grown in importance.

Despite having a coastline more than 3,000 miles (5,000 km) long and offshore waters rich in marine life, Argentines have not yet exploited the country's fishing potential. Unlike beef, fish does not form a major part of the Argentine diet.

Livestock and Crops

Since colonial times, grains such as wheat and corn were cultivated, and cattle and sheep were raised to supply export goods such as wool, animal hides, and beef. Spanish settlers first introduced cattle to Argentina in the 16th century. As animals escaped into the wild, they bred on the Pampas, until an estimated 40 million wild cattle roamed the grasslands.

The Estancia Haberton near Ushuaia on Tierra del Fuego is one of Argentina's most famous ranches.

Until the 18th century, Argentina relied on these wild cattle for everything from leather for shelter or clothing to tallow (animal fat) for candles. Later, the Spanish settlers began to domesticate the wild animals.

Goats stand in a pen on a small ranch in the Calchaquís Valley in Salta province.

During the boom years of the late 19th century, the building of a national railroad allowed foods to be transported across the country quickly. Improved methods of preserving and freezing meat also allowed more to be exported overseas. Demand for food from other countries led to Argentina planting more cereal crops and exporting more beef.

Between 1870 and 1900, the amount of land under cultivation increased fifteen-fold. Argentina encouraged immigration so that there would be enough workers for the new meat and cereal industries. Since the *estancieros*, or ranchers, already controlled most of the countryside, the new immigrants settled in Buenos Aires. When World War I broke out in 1914, Argentina produced almost half the world's total beef exports. It was also exporting wheat, corn, mutton, and wool. For many years export taxes on these products provided the government with its major source of income.

In the United States, small family farmers as well as larger landowners benefited from their country's prosperity. In Argentina, however, the best lands and most of the wealth were concentrated in the hands of a few families. The majority of the people either worked for the large *estancias* or farmed less fertile land. Even today, rural poverty remains a pressing problem in Argentina.

Argentina is still one of the world's main exporters of wheat. It also exports corn, oilseed, sorghum, soybeans, and sugar. Beef is not as important as it was. Since the

Argentina harvests almost 17.6 million tons (16 million t) of wheat per year—making it the world's tenth-biggest wheat producer.

HOW ARGENTINA USES ITS LAND

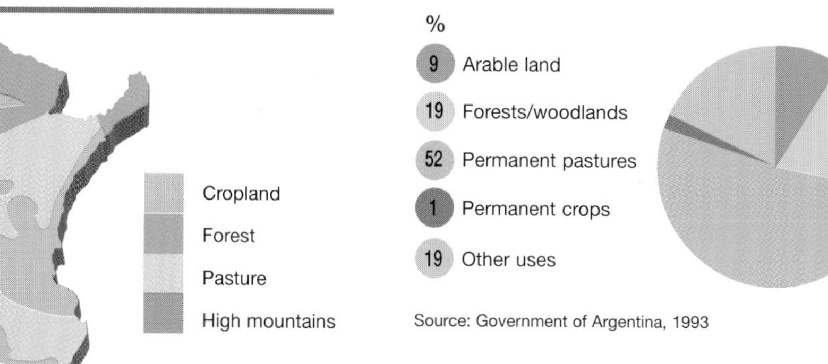

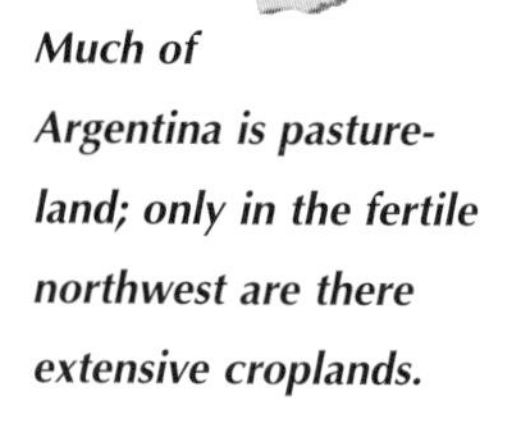

Much of Argentina is pastureland; only in the fertile northwest are there extensive croplands.

LAND USE

%	
9	Arable land
19	Forests/woodlands
52	Permanent pastures
1	Permanent crops
19	Other uses

Source: Government of Argentina, 1993

1960s, more and more farmers have switched from cattle to growing crops. Sheep, which were traditionally kept for wool, are now being raised for meat. Today more land is used for grazing sheep than anything else in the country.

Argentina's winegrowers are becoming well known for producing good-quality but affordable wine. One success has been with red wine produced from the Malbec grape, which originally came from France. Winegrowers discovered that the grape produces a higher-quality wine when grown in Argentina. Rice, fruit, olives, cotton, *yerba mate* (a green tea), and nuts are also grown for the home market. Alfalfa crops are usually used to feed cattle.

Thousands of peppers lie on the ground in the Calchaquís Valley, Salta province, during the pepper harvest.

Mineral Resources and Energy

Argentina is rich in minerals and oil. In the foothills of the Andes, there are large deposits of copper, gold, tin, lead, and iron ore. The government has recently allowed foreign companies to mine the country's gold and copper. Despite the country's name, the only mineral not found in Argentina is silver (*see* pp. 7 and 95).

Argentina is self-sufficient in energy and produces more oil, gas, and hydroelectricity than it uses. A pipeline, starting at Comodoro Rivadavia, on the Patagonian coast, carries fuel some 1,000 miles (1,600 km) to Buenos Aires. Huge dams on the country's ten main rivers, including the Paraná and Uruguay, produce hydroelectricity. Natural gas is found in Patagonia and in the northwest. Oil is extracted on land and off the southern coast of Argentina. Experts say that only one-third of Argentina's territory has been properly surveyed for oil, lead, copper, and other mineral resources (*see* pp. 117–119).

ENERGY SOURCES

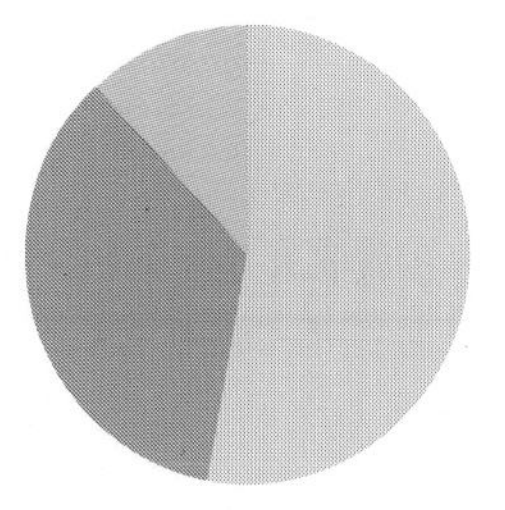

%
53 Oil, gas, coal, and diesel
35 Hydroelectricity
12 Nuclear power

Source: Government of Argentina

Argentina has rich energy resources, producing more energy than it consumes.

The First Government-owned Oil Company

The *Yacimientos Petrolíferos Fiscales* (YPF) was the world's first government-owned oil company. It was also the only one that never made a profit. Because it was the only oil company in Argentina and faced no competition, it became very inefficient.

People saw the Argentine oil company as a symbol of everything that was wrong with Argentine business. YPF employees enjoyed a guaranteed monthly salary, so some only went to work one day a month just before payday. They earned the nickname *"ñoquis,"* the name for a traditional potato pasta served in Argentine homes on the 29th of each month before payday. The YPF became so inefficient that in 1980, although enough oil to meet all of the country's needs was processed, Argentina had to import oil.

In June 1993, President Carlos Menem privatized the company, so it was run by businesspeople rather than by the government. Although the company sold for more than $3 billion, the sale was unpopular with many Argentines. They suspected that someone might be profiting illegally from it.

A truck-mounted drill is used to test for the presence of oil. Unlike Mexico, which built its manufacturing with profits from oil, Argentina has largely failed to capitalize on its rich oil fields.

Industry

Traditionally, Argentina's industries were often closely connected with its agriculture. Factories tanned animal hides or processed meat and other foods. Argentina's mineral wealth, meanwhile, went unexploited, and there was almost no manufacturing industry.

It was only with the mass immigration from Europe between 1870 and 1914 that some of the new arrivals used their knowledge to start small industrial businesses similar to the ones that they had experience with in their own countries. In 1940, manufacturing finally overtook beef as the highest domestic earner. At this time, wages were high and people wanted goods to buy. Argentine businesses were able to meet the demand, producing automobiles, refrigerators, radios, and televisions for the domestic market.

Argentina's biggest trading partner is neighboring Brazil—a fellow member of the trading bloc MERCOSUR.

President Perón (*see* pp. 69–71) tried to boost Argentina's manufacturing industry by putting high import taxes on foreign goods and making them more expensive than home-produced products. This created an artificial market in which Argentine goods had an advantage. This kind of economic policy is called "protectionism."

When the military regimes took power, they reversed Perón's protectionist measures and tried to attract more investment from other countries. After Perón's return to power in 1973, he brought back protectionism. He also introduced a policy of high wages to encourage people to buy more goods produced locally. The result of these various policies was high inflation—a dramatic rise in prices—especially during the 1970s and 1980s.

Inflation threatened to destroy Argentina's economy. The government printed more money to encourage people to buy goods and services, but the peso fell in value compared with other currencies, especially the U.S. dollar. Because Argentines preferred to buy better-quality foreign goods, the domestic market stopped growing. Argentine industry supplied only enough for the country's needs, so there was nothing to export. Prices spiraled out of control

EXPORTS

IMPORTS

EXPORTS ($bn)		IMPORTS ($bn)	
Vegetable products	4.5	Machinery	7.6
Processed foods	3.8	Chemicals	3.7
Minerals	3.1	Transport equipment	3.4
Live animals	2.2	Plastics	1.5
Oils and fats	1.9	Metals	1.5
Total (including others)	23.8	Total (including others)	22.2

Source: Government of Argentina, 1996

Argentina exports more than it imports. In 1996, it had a trade surplus of $1.6 billion.

MERCOSUR

In 1991, the "Southern Cone" countries of Argentina, Brazil, Paraguay, and Uruguay signed an economic treaty in Asunción, the Paraguayan capital. The treaty set up a special trading zone called MERCOSUR, short for *Mercado Común del Sur* ("Common Market of the South"). Chile and Bolivia became associate members of MERCOSUR in 1996 and 1997 respectively.

Eventually MERCOSUR aims to set up tariff-free trade between its members, similar to that enjoyed by the countries in the European Union (EU). Unlike the EU, however, MERCOSUR does not allow for the free movement of labor from country to country. One of the main aims of the common market is to stimulate business and trade in South America. Argentina's trade with Brazil, for example, has tripled in the 1990s as a result of both countries being members of MERCOSUR.

MERCOSUR may transform the South American economy. With a combined population of 220 million and a gross national product of U.S. $ 1.3 trillion in 1997, MERCOSUR is the fastest-growing trading bloc in the world. It experienced a trade growth of 400 percent in the period 1990–1997.

MAJOR INDUSTRIES

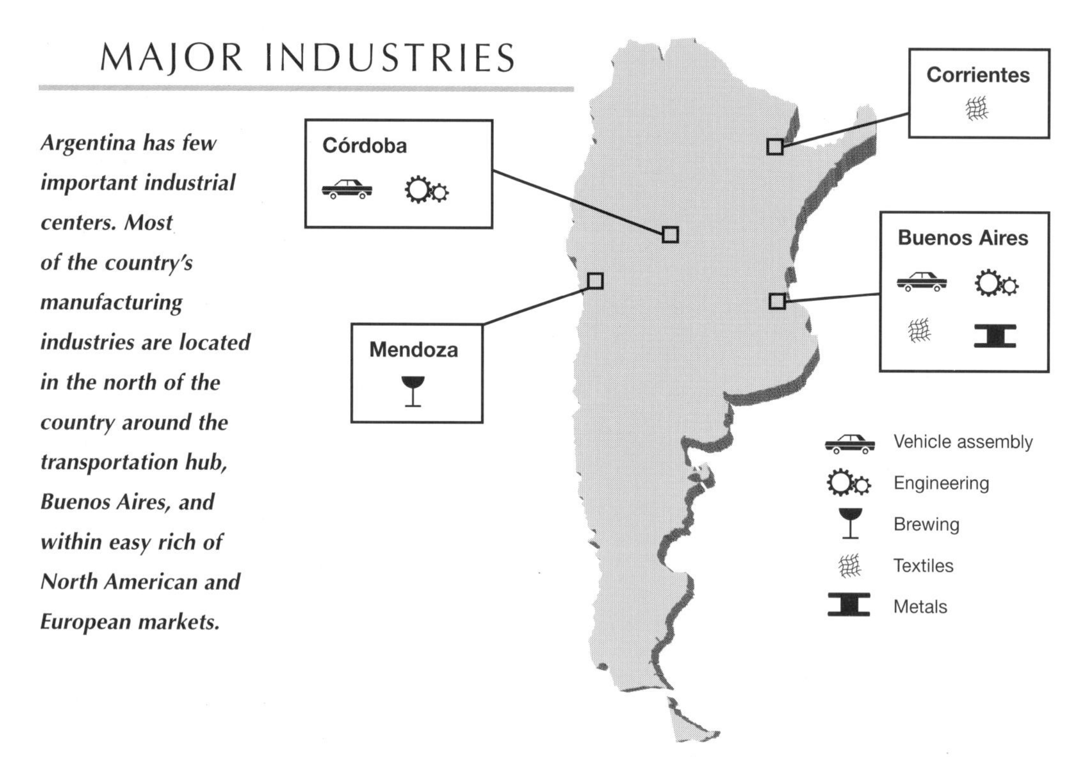

Argentina has few important industrial centers. Most of the country's manufacturing industries are located in the north of the country around the transportation hub, Buenos Aires, and within easy rich of North American and European markets.

until inflation reached 3,000 percent at the end of the 1980s. Salaries could not keep up with rising prices. Soon, many Argentines could not afford to buy anything except food and basic goods. Argentina was not the only country affected by hyperinflation: Brazil and Mexico also had this problem.

High rates of inflation has meant that Argentina has had to change currency four times in the last 50 years.

In 1992, the currency of the time, the austral, was replaced by the peso at an exchange rate of one peso to 10,000 australes. President Menem introduced strict economic policies. Many inefficient government-owned businesses were sold into private hands. In addition to the oil company (YPF), the government privatized the national telephone company, the national airline *Aerolíneas Argentinas*, the railroad network, gas, water, and power companies, the radio and part of the television networks, and even the Buenos Aires zoo.

At last, inflation seemed to be under control. In March 1995, there was actually a deflation of -0.4 percent. For the first ten months of 1998, inflation was 0.7 percent, a lower figure than most other countries.

Developing Tourism

As Argentina looks for ways to increase its income, tourism is potentially very important. Because tourists spend foreign currency buying domestic products and services, economists treat tourism as a kind of export. Today Argentina's tourist industry accounts for some 20 percent of the country's total export earnings.

In 1993, more than 3.5 million foreign tourists visited the country, bringing in $3.6 billion. The largest number of tourists from outside South America came from France, followed by North America, Spain, and Italy. People from Argentina's nearest neighbors, Brazil, Chile, Paraguay, and Uruguay, also visit the country frequently.

Top tourist attractions include trips to the Iguazú Falls, skiing and hiking in the Lake District, and visiting the beaches of Mar del Plata, Argentina's vacation capital. Some *estancias* take in paying guests to make extra money. The guests share daily life on the ranch, helping with the horses, and enjoying the traditional *parrillada*—a mixed grill of Argentine meat.

Tourism is a big employer in Argentina, too. More than half a million people work in the industry, providing services for Argentine and international tourists.

MAIN FOREIGN ARRIVALS

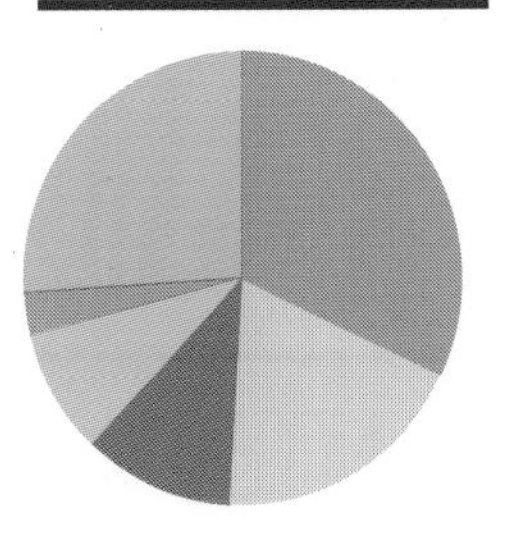

%
- 32 Uruguay
- 19 Chile
- 11 Brazil
- 9 Paraguay
- 3 Bolivia
- 26 Others

Source: Government of Argentina

Most visitors to Argentina come from neighboring countries in South America.

Tourists crowd a beach in Mar del Plata, Buenos Aires province. In summer, the city's population swells to three times its normal number as Argentines take their vacations.

Troubled Times

By 1995, unemployment had risen to more than 18 percent. This was because of a large reduction in the number of government employees and a general drive for efficiency in business. Poverty grew and hunger became commonplace in a country that has always prided itself on being self-sufficient in food. At this time, some 9 million Argentines lived in poverty.

A large international debt (the amount of money one country owes other countries in loans) also contributed to the economic problems. When its international debt stood at $62 billion, experts estimated that Argentina would have to pay all its foreign export earnings for 27 months to cancel the debt. In 1996, the debt stood at a staggering $93.8 billion.

TRANSPORTATION

Because Argentina's population is concentrated in and around the capital, Buenos Aires, most transportation routes lead to and from the capital. The first great transportation links were the railroads built in the late 19th century. In the 20th century, road and air links became more important than railroads, both for passenger travel and transportation of freight.

A passenger boards a bus in Bariloche, in the Argentine Lake District. Local or **común** ***bus services provide inexpensive transportation around towns and cities. Unlike intercity or*** **expreso** ***buses they make frequent stops and are often crowded.***

TRANSPORTATION

Argentina has one of the most extensive transportation systems in South America. Most major roads and railroads fan out from the capital, Buenos Aires. The south of Argentina, particularly Patagonia, is less well served by rail and road connections. Most surface freight is transported by road, although coastal cities are served by small ships that also carry passengers. Air travel is expensive, but is often the best way of getting to small, remote centers such as Ushuaia at the southern tip of the country.

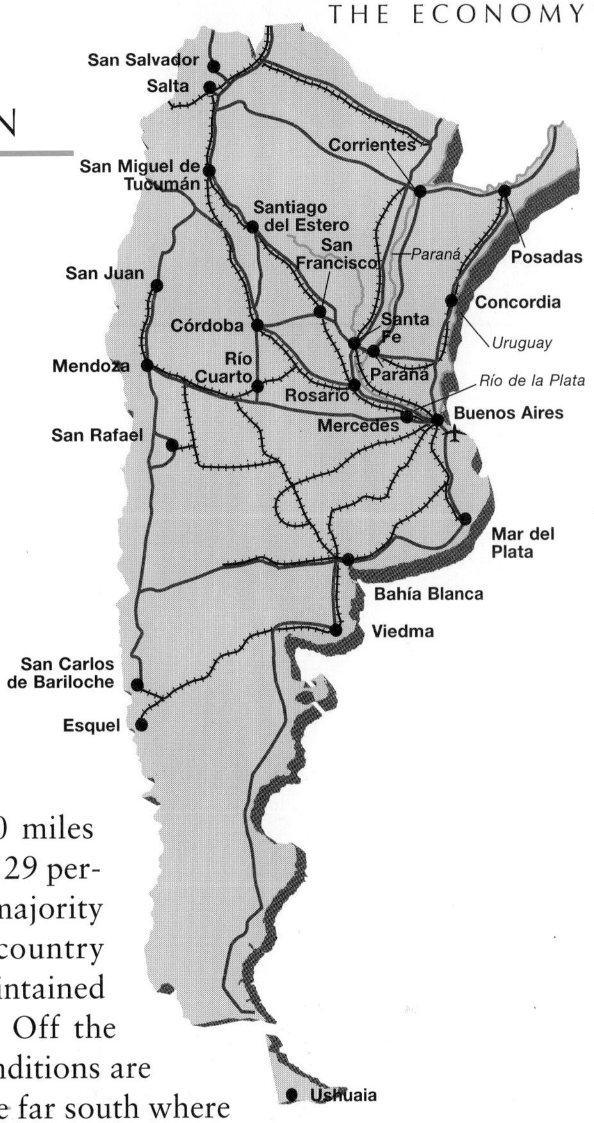

major highways
railroads
major waterways
major airport

Highways and Roads

Argentina has almost 134,000 miles (215,650 km) of road, but only 29 percent of the total is paved. The majority consists of dirt roads. Crosscountry highways are well built and maintained and are usually not crowded. Off the main routes, however, road conditions are often not good, especially in the far south where roads may be impassable in winter. The country's most famous highway is Route 40 (*see* p. 88).

For people who cannot afford to travel Argentina's long distances by air, there is an extensive network of air-conditioned buses that covers the entire country. The buses are often comfortable, with televisions, snacks, and drinks, but the journey times can be extremely long. To travel from Buenos Aires to Ushuaia—the town farthest south in Argentina—takes ten times as long by road as by air. It is a three-hour plane ride and a 30-hour road journey. The bus does have one advantage over the plane—it costs much less.

Argentina has a poor road-safety record. In 1994, 1,200 people died in road accidents for every million vehicles on the road—five times the level in the United States.

Rail, Sea, and Air

In 1998, the national railroad network extended for 23,556 miles (37,910 km). Many of the railroads were financed and built by the British in the mid-19th century, and they made an important contribution to Argentina's prosperity in this period. The railroad was bought up by the national government in 1948.

There were railroads in the Pampas before there were roads. The soil-bed was too wet for road building, and it was easier to lay rail tracks. Small towns sprang up next to railroad stations.

By the early 1990s, when the railroads were resold to private companies, less than half of the network was operational. Today only 10 percent of the total goods transported in Argentina go by rail, and fewer than 10 percent of passengers choose the train, even though it is cheaper than the bus. By 1998, there were very few trains left outside of the Buenos Aires area.

The Subte (*see* pp. 37–38), the subway network in Buenos Aires, is the oldest in Latin America, dating back to 1913. Some 800,000 people use the system each weekday. Until 1991, the subway was not very reliable, and there were frequent breakdowns. The system is now being modernized with Japanese subway cars, although some of the original cars are still in use.

Argentina has four main seaports: Buenos Aires (*see* box opposite), La Plata, Rosario, and Bahía Blanca. A regular ferry along the Paraná River connects Argentina and Paraguay. Ferries and hydrofoils cross the Río de la Plata to Colonia in Uruguay for travel from Buenos Aires to Uruguay, with bus-service links with Montevideo.

Route 40

Argentina's most famous road, Route 40, is comparable to the Trans-Alaska Highway in North America. It runs almost the entire length of Argentina, from the Bolivian border in the north to near the southern tip of Tierra del Fuego. The road is more than 3,100 miles (5,000 km) long.

Only one-third of Route 40 is paved; the rest is dirt. The road passes through every climate zone in Argentina and climbs to a height of more than 16,000 feet (4,875 m). Driving Route 40 is a popular vacation trip for Argentines, but they need to make the trip in a four-wheel-drive vehicle because of the uneven road surfaces, especially in Patagonia.

Although it is expensive, air travel is often the easiest way of traveling throughout Argentina. Because of the importance of Buenos Aires in national life, most internal flights operate in and out of the capital.

Argentina is connected by direct international flights to the rest of the world, but because the country is so far south, most flights take a long time. It takes more than 16 hours to fly from Los Angeles to Buenos Aires, and more than 14 from New York. It is quicker to fly to Moscow from New York, or to Tokyo from Los Angeles.

The Buenos Aires Docks

Since the late 18th century, the Buenos Aires docks have played a key part in Argentina's history and economy. The port's closeness to the fertile Pampas made it ideal for the export of the region's meat and and hides. The port's busy wharfs and the colorful district of La Boca were usually the first glimpse that immigrants had of their adopted country.

Like many Argentine cities along the Atlantic coast, Buenos Aires had long been able to receive only small freighters. In the 1920s, however, the port was enlarged, and Buenos Aires became the first Argentine port to handle large container ships. Today 96 percent of the country's container traffic passes through the port. Forty percent of Argentina's total international trade is connected with the docks. More than 60 maritime companies use the port, and some 70 ships arrive and leave each week.

adidas
22
18

Arts and Living

"When all is said and done, the tango is nothing less than a reflection of our daily reality."

Edmundo Rivero, one of Argentina's great tango singers

People sometimes describe Argentina as the most European of Latin American cultures. The first Spanish settlers destroyed almost every trace of the native Indians' way of life, and instead developed a society and culture that looked back across the Atlantic to their "home" country in Spain. Argentine art, architecture, and writing modeled themselves on those of Europe. Even today, the capital, Buenos Aires, with its broad avenues and lively cafés, has a strong resemblance to European cities, such as Paris or Barcelona.

It was only in the 19th century, after Argentina won its independence, that a special Argentine culture began to develop. In Buenos Aires, thinkers and writers debated what made Argentina different from other Spanish cultures and in what direction it ought to develop. Mass immigration from Europe in the 19th century also had a major influence on Argentine culture. The famous Argentine music and dance form known as the tango was born in a multiethnic Buenos Aires. Outside the capital, an oral tradition of storytelling and singing developed as gaucho poets traveled from settlement to settlement, singing about the joys and troubles of their daily lives.

In the 20th century, Argentina's literary culture and movie industry have both enjoyed periods of great activity and growth. However, they have also been censored and controlled by the country's many military dictators.

The Argentine soccer team play against Japan in the 1998 World Cup in France. The blue and white Argentine uniform reflects the national flag.

FACT FILE

- Buenos Aires has 16 museums and some 40 theaters, including the world-famous opera house, the Teatro Colón.
- The world's first animated movie—*El Apóstol* ("The Apostle")—was made in Argentina in 1917.
- British sailors first introduced the game of soccer to Argentina in the 1840s. The first Argentine team was founded in 1897.
- Argentina's most famous music and dance form, the tango, was first developed in the poor areas of Buenos Aires, known collectively as the *arrabal*.

ARTS

For a long time, the arts of Argentina followed the example of Europe and especially Spain. Architects, sculptors, painters, and writers worked in the styles of their Spanish counterparts. Only in the late 19th and 20th centuries, as Argentina struggled to form a national identity, did truly Argentine styles begin to emerge.

Building Cities: Cathedrals, Parks, and Monuments

Unlike the Inca of Peru or the Aztec and Maya of Mexico, the nomadic peoples of Argentina built hardly any cities or monumental buildings. Only in the far northwest of the country, where Indians set up permanent settlements, are there important remains of buildings. The most impressive is the ruined fortress of Quilmes, built in about A.D. 1000 by the Quilmes Indians (*see* p. 45).

The country's oldest buildings to survive intact date from the time when the Spanish ruled the country. They built fine churches and town and city halls (*cabildos*) in the popular styles of their own country. Often the buildings were made of *adobe*—sun-baked earth and straw—and then white-washed. The city of Salta in the northwest Andes is one of the best-preserved colonial cities in Argentina (*see* p. 24).

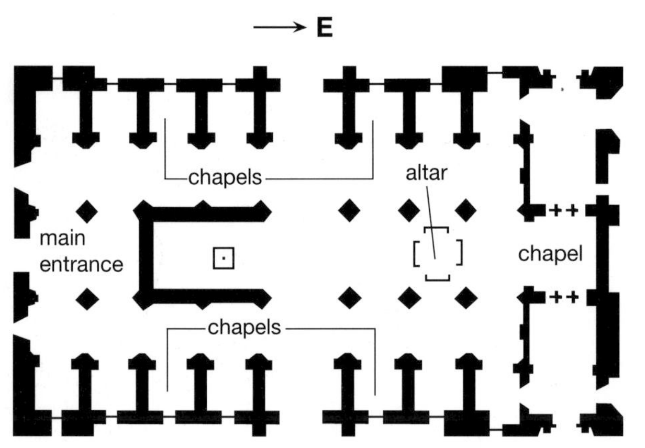

Argentine churches and cathedrals are often very ornate. Inside, chapels have magnificent painted and carved altarpieces called retables.

In the late 19th century, Argentina's capital, Buenos Aires, was reorganized using Paris as its model. The Plaza de Mayo, which had been full of garbage and market stalls, was cleared and grassed over. The presidential palace, the Casa Rosada, was finished in a French style, and streets were widened into grand tree-lined avenues. Owing to the many beautiful, European-style buildings that were built at this time, the city became known as the "Paris of the South."

Porteños like to stroll through Buenos Aires's Botanical Garden (Jardín Botánico), in the barrio of Palermo. with its beautiful trees, plants, and fountains.

Some people think that the appearance of Argentina's cities owes more to its parks and gardens than to its buildings. Architects who design gardens, parks, and other open spaces in cities are called landscape architects. Landscape architect Charles Thays filled the centers of Argentina's plazas with flourishing gardens. He designed parks in the capital as well as in Córdoba and Tucumán. His greatest work, however, is Buenos Aires's Botanical Garden. Thays wanted to create a garden that could express the Argentines' pride in their country, so he traveled throughout the country looking for native plants to grow in the gardens.

Today Argentina has no distinct architectural movement, and recent buildings are often large and impersonal. Like many Western cities, Buenos Aires's skyline is a mixture of older buildings and shiny skyscrapers.

National Monuments

The Argentines often celebrate the important events and people of their history by erecting public monuments in city squares, streets, and parks. Many towns and cities have statues of the two greatest heroes of independence, General Belgrano (*see* p. 59) and San Martín. In a park in Mendoza, for example, a huge stone block is decorated with scenes showing San Martín's army crossing the Andes. Other monuments recall Argentina's great writers and musicians (*see* p. 98). For Argentina, as for many other countries, monuments are an important way in which the nation can express its identity and show pride in its history.

Painting and Sculpture

The early Indian inhabitants of Argentina have left little trace of their art. In Patagonia, there are beautiful cave paintings of animals such as the guanaco and of human hands (*see* p. 48) in bright reds, oranges, black, and white. In northwest Argentina, in the foothills of the Andes, are standing stones, or menhirs. Some menhirs are carved or sculpted and form part of stone circles.

In 19th-century Argentina, architects and painters looked to Europe, especially France, for inspiration. Wealthy Argentines considered everything European civilized and saw native art as "barbaric." They traveled to Europe to see the work of European painters and brought home their paintings to hang in their houses.

To sell their work, Argentine painters had to copy the styles of European painters. They produced work influenced by major European art movements such as Neoclassicism, Impressionism, and Realism. Until the 20th century, it was difficult for a truly Argentine art to establish itself.

There are 129 standing stones in the Parque de los Menires in the Tafí Valley in Tucumán. Experts think that the valley was an important sacred place for the local Indians. The standing stones may have represented gods or spirits, who protected the tribe from harm.

"The Country of Silver"

The Inca of South America had a long tradition of silver mining and silver work. Their mines lay high up in the freezing Andes, in modern Bolivia. Local peasants were drafted into laboring in the mines.

The legendary wealth of the Inca motivated the Spanish to explore the continent. They seized the Inca mines and dug new ones of their own. They also adopted the Inca working system. In 1545, they discovered the richest silver deposits in the Americas—the Cerro Rico at Potosí. Every year, some 13,000 Indians from villages in the central Andes were pressed into forced labor in the Potosí silver mine. In 1776, the mines became part of the new Viceroyalty of Río de la Plata ("River of Silver"), which later became Argentina—"the country of silver."

Buenos Aires became an important center for silver work. In 1700, there were already 38 silversmiths working in the city. Silver was used to make beautiful lamps and chalices for churches and silver cutlery for wealthy *porteños*, while gauchos proudly wore silver-handled daggers, or *facones*.

Gradually silver fell out of fashion. People wanted the china and glass that was imported from Europe. Today only a few silversmiths work in Buenos Aires.

Immigration created a lively cultural mix in Buenos Aires, attracting many would-be artists from the rest of Argentina to the capital. Martín Fierro—named after a famous poem by the Argentine writer José Hernández (*see* p. 94)—was an avant-garde (experimental) artistic movement of the 1920s that included both writers and artists. The best-known Martín Fierro artist was Xul Solar (1887–1963), who illustrated many of the works of writer Jorge Luis Borges (*see* p. 98). Solar was very eccentric and even invented his own languages.

During Perón's presidency, artists found their work condemned if it did not appeal to the people. It was only in the 1960s that artists enjoyed greater freedom. An art scene developed in Buenos Aires, centered on an area known as *manzana loca*, or "crazy block." However, the military dictatorships harassed artists, too, and closed down art galleries and studios. Since the restoration of democracy, Argentine art is slowly reviving.

One of Argentina's most famous artists is Benito Quinquela Martín, who painted pictures of La Boca in Buenos Aires.

Payadores

One of Argentina's oldest forms of literature is the poem-songs of the *payadores.* The *payadores* were wandering gaucho singers who engaged in musical duels known as *payadas.* Accompanying himself on the guitar, each *payador* would try to outdo the other in improvising music and words. *Payador* songs might be about historical or contemporary events. Although the *payadores* did not write their songs down, they had a powerful influence on both Argentine writing and music.

Literature and the Gaucho

Argentina began to create its own literature at the time of independence. People wrote patriotic poems and political works as part of the campaign for independence. After independence, leading writers such as Esteban Echeverría (1805–1851) debated the new country's future in literary salons in Buenos Aires. Introduced from Europe, the literary salon was a social gathering, usually in someone's home, where intellectuals, thinkers, poets, and writers could discuss the important issues.

Writers such as Echeverría and Domingo Faustimo Sarmiento (1811–1888) opposed the Rosas dictatorship. Writing in exile in Chile, Sarmiento published *Facundo: Civilization and Barbarism* (1845), in which he attacked the dictatorship. In his work, Sarmiento suggested that the country could only mature by adopting European political and social ideas. For Sarmiento, the gaucho was a symbol of all that was backward-looking in Argentina. Sarmiento later became president of Argentina.

An answer to Sarmiento's text came from a landowner, José Hernández (1834–1886), who wrote *El Gaucho Martín Fierro* ("The

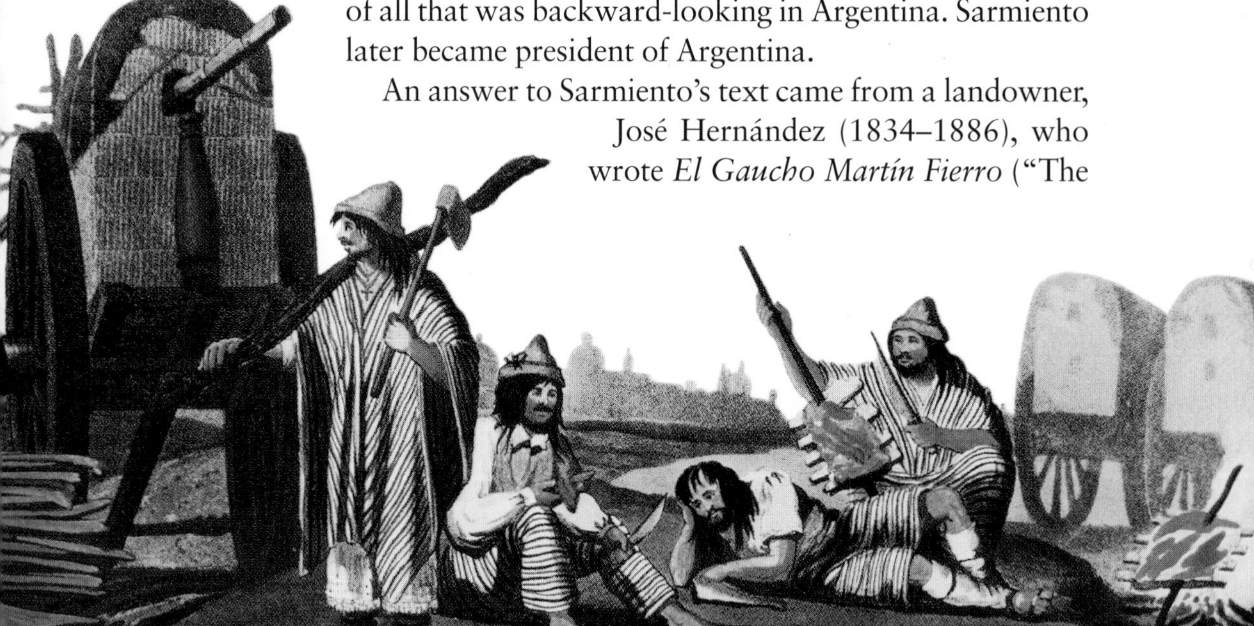

In the 19th century, writers debated the merits of the gaucho lifestyle. Some praised it for its romantic freedom, while others criticized its backwardness.

Gaucho Martín Fierro"; 1872) in the form of a gaucho *payada* song (*see* box opposite). The poem tells the story of a gaucho who is conscripted into the army and becomes a deserter and outlaw. The sequel, *La Vuelta de Martín Fierro* ("The Return of Martín Fierro"; 1879), shows how Martín Fierro comes to terms with society.

Hernández wanted his books to be a protest against the modernization of Argentina and, in particular, against the development of city culture. He portrayed the gaucho as the hero of traditional Argentine life rather than the villain. The way that Hernández described gaucho life made it seem so romantic that his hero, Martín Fierro, came to symbolize the Argentine nation.

Writing for Writing's Sake

The economic boom that started in the 1880s was a turning point for Argentine literature. For the first time, there were professional writers who thought of themselves primarily as writers rather than as politicians or landowners who also wrote. Their inspiration was a Nicaraguan poet, Rubén Darío (1867–1916), who also lived in Argentina for a time. Darío led a movement called *modernismo* ("modernism"), which asserted that poetry was an art form and not a vehicle for expressing political ideas or teaching people something. This notion is sometimes called "art for art's sake."

In the early part of the 20th century, Argentine literature continued to build on Darío's work. Literary magazines such as *Martín Fierro* championed poetry and criticized the political writings and memoirs so common in Argentina in the 1920s.

It was at this time that Argentina's most famous writer, Jorge Luis Borges (1899–1986), began his literary career. Borges's writing shows how many Argentines are not sure whether they belong to South America or Europe. Not only do the short stories that Borges wrote reflect this conflict; his life, too, was an example of the close link between Argentina and Europe.

"The composition of vast books is a laborious and impoverishing extravagance... A better course of action is to pretend that these books already exist, and then to offer a resumé, a commentary... and notes upon [them]."
Jorge Borges

Many of the most influential writings and poetry of the 1930s and 1940s first appeared in another literary journal—*Sur* ("South")—founded by the writer Victoria Ocampo (1890–1979). Borges and several other writers used the magazine to discuss their literary ideas. The writers rejected the nationalism and realism typical of Argentine literature in the 19th century and experimented with different styles and techniques. Argentine literature had begun to find its own voice.

Jorge Luis Borges

Argentina's most famous writer was born in Buenos Aires in 1899. His father's large library of English books was a constant reminder of the family's British ancestry, of which Borges was always very proud. Borges left for Europe with his family at the age of 15 in 1914 and returned to Buenos Aires only in 1921. The long trip gave Borges the opportunity to study the work of modern European authors and to begin writing himself.

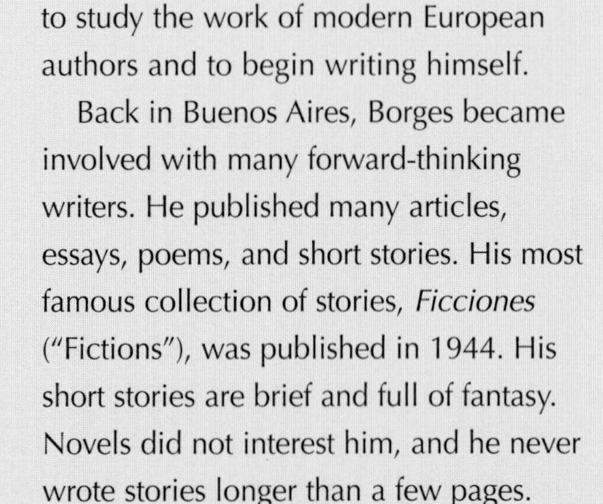

Back in Buenos Aires, Borges became involved with many forward-thinking writers. He published many articles, essays, poems, and short stories. His most famous collection of stories, *Ficciones* ("Fictions"), was published in 1944. His short stories are brief and full of fantasy. Novels did not interest him, and he never wrote stories longer than a few pages.

Although Borges hated Juan Perón and his ideas, he nevertheless stayed in Argentina during Perón's presidency. In 1955, after Perón left the country, Borges became director of the National Library. By now, he was blind, and he started to compose poetry again, thinking it through in his head before dictating it. In the 1970s, he published more short stories. He died in Geneva, Switzerland, in 1986. This monument to Borges stands in Palermo Park in Buenos Aires.

Writing under Dictatorship

During the dictatorship of Juan Perón (1946–1955), Argentine literature suffered a severe setback. Perón associated most Argentine writers with the liberal ideas he sought to attack and suppressed their writings. Many writers, such as Julio Cortázar (1914–1984), went into voluntary exile.

In the 1960s, a mood of excitement and experimentation swept Argentina in the arts. Cortázar returned from exile in France, and, in 1963, he published *Rayuela* ("Hopscotch"). The novel follows the story of an Argentine living in Paris who returns to Buenos Aires. This period of artistic freedom was cut short by the military coup of 1966, when writing all but stopped. Writers were targets for the military and many "disappeared." Manuel Puig (1932–1990) was forced to live abroad, and his books were banned in Argentina. He is mainly famous outside Argentina for his 1976 novel about a political prisoner, *El Beso de la Mujer Araña* ("The Kiss of the Spiderwoman").

It was only with the return of civilian rule in 1983 that writers regained freedom of expression. In the 1990s, there was another boom in Argentine literature. One of the most successful writers at this time was Tomás Eloy Martinez (born 1934), who enjoyed international recognition with the publication of *La Novela de Perón* and *Santa Evita*. The latter is a half-fictional, half-factual account of how Argentine military dictators had Eva Perón's body taken to Europe so that she could not be buried in Argentina.

"Sierra"

Alfonsina Storni (1892–1938) is one of Argentina's greatest poets. She grew up in the provinces of San Juan and Santa Fe and became a teacher and a journalist. She published her first book of poetry to great acclaim in 1916. In 1938, Storni discovered that she was incurably sick and drowned herself in the sea at the popular seaside resort of Mar del Plata. In this excerpt from her poem "Sierra," Storni evokes the landscapes of Argentina. The reference to August snow is less strange than it first appears—August is a winter month in Argentina.

An invisible hand
silently caresses
the sad pulp
of the rolling worlds.

Someone, I don't know who,
has steeped my heart
in sweetness.

In the August snow
the blossom of the peach
tree—
early flowering—
opens to the sun.

"It takes two to tango." A man and woman perform Argentina's national dance in a street in Buenos Aires. Couples dance in a close embrace, with the man leading the woman. Some people say that the tango reflects the machismo (male-dominated) culture of Argentina.

Playing, Dancing, and Singing the Tango

The national music and dance of Argentina is the tango. The music first developed in the poor slum areas—the *arrabal*—of Buenos Aires toward the end of the 19th century. Nobody is certain about the exact origins of tango. Historians generally agree, however, that it arose out of a fusion of many different musical cultures, including Spanish flamenco, African dance rhythms, and the music of the gaucho troubadours.

Experts also debate where the word "tango" actually comes from. Some say that it comes from the old Spanish word *tañer*, meaning "to play an instrument." Others believe it is an African word for "dance."

The earliest tango music was played in the bars where newly arrived immigrants went to enjoy themselves. The passionate style of tango music expressed both the sense of loss and nostalgia that immigrants felt at leaving their countries behind and their hope for the future, however uncertain it was.

The notes above show the typical basic rhythm of the tango—slow-quick-slow-slow.

When the tango began, it was only instrumental. Common instruments used were the piano, violin, guitar, and flute. Another popular tango instrument was a kind of large accordion called the *bandoneón*, which was imported from Germany. *Bandoneones* are no longer made, so the old ones are carefully maintained.

As the music became more popular, people began to add dance steps to the music. The tango dance, as it is known the world over, was born. The tango became respectable and highly fashionable in Argentina only after it had become popular in France. When the Argentine middle and upper classes realized how popular the dance had become in Paris—then the most fashionable city in the world—they quickly forgot about its origins in working-class bars and started to tango!

The next major change in tango came in 1910 when lyrics were added to the music. Words made the emotions expressed even more obvious. The song "*Mi noche triste*" ("My Sad Night") composed by Samuel Castriota in 1915, turned tango from dance music into song. People all over Latin America were able to listen to it thanks to the phonograph, an early form of recorded music player. The great Carlos Gardel (*see* p. 102) co-wrote many of the songs that today are still considered tango classics. Tango songs always mixed love and longing, but by the

"My Beloved Buenos Aires"

One of Carlos Gardel's most famous and best-loved tango songs is "Mi Buenos Aires querido" ("My Beloved Buenos Aires"). In this song, Gardel expresses his homesickness for his native city.

My beloved Buenos Aires
When I see you next
There will be no more pain or forgotten times.
The lamp on the street where I was born
was the sentinel
Of my promises of love, under the still light
I saw her,
My shining darling, like the sun.
Destiny desires that I see you again, port city,
The only one for me.

Carlos Gardel

Carlos Gardel (1887–1935) is the most famous of all tango artists. He was born in France in 1887, but at the age of three, his mother brought him to Buenos Aires. where he grew up among the poor immigrant *porteños.* As a young man, he scraped out a living by doing odd jobs. At night, he entertained his neighbors with his passionate songs of lost love and homesickness.

Gardel first gained success with his singing partner, José Razzano. When Razzano lost his voice, Gardel went solo. He became a star not only in Argentina but throughout Latin America. His voice, good looks, and charisma made him a very successful performer and recording artist and later a movie star. Gardel died suddenly in 1935, in a plane crash in Colombia.

After his death, Gardel became even more popular. His tomb in the Chacarita Cemetery in Buenos Aires remains a place of pilgrimage for tango fans. Pictures of Gardel, smiling and dressed in a suit and wearing a British-style soft-felt hat known as a trilby and a white scarf around his neck, are still a common sight in Buenos Aires, where he is known as *El Zorzal Criollo*—the "creole songbird."

1930s, the songs had become increasingly sad. They told of the difficulties of life in Argentina, the years of depression, and the failed expectations of many of the poorer immigrants.

In the 1940s and 1950s, tango became a lively dance music that everyone listened to on the radio at home. President Juan Perón promoted tango as part of Argentina's national culture, and Perón's supporters tried to use the tango as propaganda when he returned to power in 1973. Because they insisted that it be played on the radio and television, it made tango music seem more popular than it was.

Older Argentines still love the tango, and connoisseurs in search of the real thing go to the bars near the port and in working-class districts of Buenos Aires. Tango shows in expensive clubs in the center of Buenos Aires are for tourists. There is a radio station that plays tango 24 hours a day, and most taxi drivers play tango in their cabs. Today some younger Argentines are learning to tango.

"Gardel sings better every day." Argentine saying.

At the Movies

The Argentines love going to the movies. At the moviegoing peak in the 1920s and 1930s, there were 1,608 movie theaters across Argentina, with as many as 200 in the Buenos Aires area alone. That number has fallen, but there are still more than 70 movie theaters in the capital.

Around 90 percent of the movies shown are from Hollywood, and Argentines are keen to see all the latest releases from both the United States and Europe. Argentina also has its own film industry. As with other arts, moviemakers were censored and controlled by the military governments, but since the return to democracy the industry has grown.

Argentina won its first Oscar in 1986 for best foreign film with Luis Puenzo's *La historia oficial* ("The Official Version"), which revealed the hidden story of the military dictatorship through the story of a "Mother of the Plaza de Mayo" who tries to discover the truth about the "disappearance" of her pregnant daughter. Ten percent of the women who "disappeared" during the Dirty War were pregnant. When their children were born, they were not given back to their real families but secretly given away to families connected to the military.

Argentines go to a showing of* El Beso de la Mujer Araña *("Kiss of the Spider Woman") in Buenos Aires. Although the film is based on an Argentine novel by Manuel Puig, the film was made in Brazil.

Some Argentine gauchos continue to live in the traditional way. They live in simple, wooden houses, with a stove to keep them warm and a dog to keep them company.

EVERYDAY LIFE

Life in Argentina's cities is very different from that of the countryside. People who live in Buenos Aires consider themselves part of the modern, international world, linked to the United States or Europe by similar lifestyles. The rural population, which lives mainly in the interior of the country, preserves a traditional lifestyle involved with farming. They do not think that they have anything in common with the people who live in Buenos Aires. They feel that they have closer links to their neighbors in Chile, Brazil, and Bolivia.

Food and Drink

Argentines usually eat three meals a day. Breakfast is light, usually coffee or *mate* and toast or croissants with butter and jam. Argentines call croissants *medialunas*, which means "half-moon," because of the shape. Lunch is often the main meal of the day and is eaten between 1:00 and 3:00 P.M. Late afternoon tea (*té*) is like breakfast and is eaten mostly by children. Dinner is eaten very late, never before 9:00 P.M. and usually at about 10:00 P.M.

People take meals very seriously in Argentina. Whether they are eating at home or in a restaurant, Argentines take their time over a meal, using it as an opportunity to discuss family matters or the day's events. Restaurant owners expect their customers to spend hours at the table and would not dream of asking them to leave.

Grilled beef from Argentina's famous cattle is a favorite food. It was so plentiful in the 19th century that

Dulce de Leche

The Argentines are very fond of Italian-style ice creams, and there are usually lots of flavors to choose from. Argentines particularly like to eat vanilla ice cream with *dulce de leche*, a specialty dessert of sweetened, caramelized milk.

Dulce de leche is a delicious dessert that can be eaten on its own, with ice cream, caramel custard, or fresh fruit. It can also be spread on bread or *alfajores*, special Argentine cookies. The usual ingredients are milk, sugar, and vanilla. The recipe below is the easiest way of making it. Ask an adult to help you.

You will need:
One can of sweetened, condensed milk, with a couple of holes punched into the lid

Method:
Put a pot of water to boil on the stove. When the water reaches boiling point, turn the heat down low and carefully set the unopened can of condensed milk into the pot. Let the milk simmer gently in the pot for two hours. Keep checking to make sure there is enough water in the pot, adding more when necessary. After two hours, turn off the heat and allow the water and can to cool completely.

When the can is cool, open it and pour the contents into a dish. It will be a rich caramel color and very thick in consistency. Serve it on its own, or with croissants, cookies, or ice cream.

A gaucho barbecues beef steaks on a ranch in the Pampas. Although Argentines eat less beef today than they did in the past, beef dishes are still very popular.

bars used to give it away as a free snack, and it was not uncommon for people to eat beef twice a day. Today people may eat it once a day, usually served with fries and salad.

Another popular dish is a *parrillada*, a mixed grill of steak and other cuts, which might include *riñones* (kidneys) and *chinchulines* (small intestines). To spice up a *parrillada*, the Argentines sometimes like to eat a fresh barbecue sauce of tomatoes, onions, green peppers, paprika, mustard, vinegar, and oil. Another sauce called *chimichurri*, made with oil, vinegar, paprika, garlic, and herbs, is left for four or five days so the flavor can develop before serving with meat.

Beef is also used for preparing *carbonada criolla*, a very rich stew that includes onion, tomatoes, sweet potatoes, potatoes, pumpkin, or squash. The final touch is

Mate Tea

The preparation and drinking of *mate* tea in Argentina is one of the few traditions to survive from pre-Columbian times. *Yerba mate* is a green herb, originally from Paraguay. Like tea, the herb is dried and powdered, and then drunk as an infusion. Preparing *mate* is a ritual. The *mate* is made in a gourd and then sipped through a special metal straw (*bombilla*), which is sometimes made out of silver. People often share a *mate*. When a person has drunk some, he or she passes the container clockwise to a neighbor, and so on. Everyone uses the same straw. On average, Argentines drink four times as much mate as coffee. They consider it to be very good for their health.

some peaches and pears and corn. Sometimes *carbonada* is served in a hollowed pumpkin.

Because of Argentina's large Italian population, pizza and pasta such as lasagne, spaghetti, and cannelloni are widely eaten. Gnocchi, or *ñoquis*, in the Argentine Spanish spelling, are a kind of potato pasta. It is an inexpensive dish that restaurants traditionally serve on the 29th of the month when money is short just before payday. When times are hard, people joke that "this month we'll have *ñoquis* on the 15th." Pizza can be eaten by the slice, and in many pizzerias it is cheaper to eat standing at the counter than sitting at a table. Pizzerias in Buenos Aires rival those in New York City.

If *porteños* get hungry between meals, they may go to a café. Buenos Aires has many cafés, such as the famous Café Tortoni on the Avenida de Mayo. The Café Tortoni was traditionally popular among artists and writers, who gathered there to discuss the latest ideas. Cafés provide tasty snacks such as *empanadas*, pastries filled with ground beef, onions, hard-boiled egg, and olives.

HOW ARGENTINES SPEND THEIR MONEY

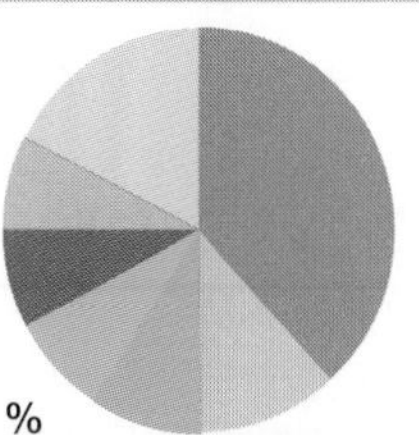

%

38 Food and drink
12 Transportation
9 Housing
8 Clothing
8 Health
8 Recreation/culture
17 Other

The Argentines spend the biggest proportion of their income on food.

Religion and Festivals

The official religion of Argentina is Roman Catholicism, and more than 90 percent of the population is Roman Catholic. The church is still very powerful in Argentina and plays a large role in the nation's life.

Critics of the church in Argentina say that it is very conservative, meaning that it works against change even when such change might bring about an improvement in conditions for the poor. They point out that during the military dictatorships, some members of the church supported the military, despite the persecution, kidnapping, and murder of religious workers alongside so many other citizens.

On the other hand, some factions of the Roman Catholic church have fought hard for social change and justice. They work in the shantytowns—the *villas miserias*—of Buenos Aires and in poor rural districts.

The Cult of Difunta Correa

In Argentina, as throughout Latin America, a wide variety of beliefs flourishes alongside the official teachings of the Roman Catholic church. The most famous unofficial cult in the country is that of *la Difunta Correa*—"the departed Correa." According to legend, Deolinda Correa was the devoted wife of an Argentine conscript during the civil wars of the 1840s. Carrying her baby with her, she followed her husband on his battalion's campaigns through the deserts of San Juan. Eventually she ran out of food and water and died in the desert. Passing travelers found her dead body but were amazed to discover that her baby still suckled at her breast. The suckling child was only the first of a series of miracles attributed to Difunta Correa. The Roman Catholic church does not recognize her as a saint. Instead, believers venerate her as a dead "soul."

The legendary site of Deolinda Correa's death is today marked with a colorful shrine. Every year, some 700,000 pilgrims come from all over Argentina to pay homage at the shrine. Easter is a particularly busy time. People leave offerings such as bank bills, flowers, and lighted candles, and ask Correa to intercede on their behalf. Correa is especially venerated by truck drivers, who sometimes even leave registration plates at the shrine.

Argentines also take spiritualism seriously and have a strong respect for the dead. For example, they do not remember the birth dates of their national heroes but the date they died. For example, the August 17 national holiday celebrates the anniversary of the death of José de San Martín. There is a steady flow of pilgrims to the two main cemeteries in Buenos Aires, where many national heroes are buried, because they believe it is important to recall the dead by leaving offerings at their graves.

Altogether Argentina has ten national holidays (*see* box). Some of these, such as Christmas and Easter, mark religious festivals. Many others celebrate important events in Argentine history such as independence. Columbus Day, celebrated throughout the Spanish world, recalls Columbus's discovery of America, while Malvinas Day recalls the foundation of an Argentine government-in-exile of the Malvinas/Falklands in 1829.

In addition to public holidays, Argentina's different provinces and cities have their own local festivals that take place throughout the year. Mendoza celebrates the grape harvest with a festival in March (*see* p. 25). In August, there is a snow festival in the small mountain town of Río Turbio in Patagonia. The town of Junín de los Andes, known as the trout capital of Argentina, holds a trout festival in December.

On national holidays, there are big parades in Buenos Aires that end at the Plaza de Mayo. On New Year's Eve, crowds stuff long paper streamers into passing cars

National Holidays

Argentina has ten national holidays, during which all businesses and government offices are closed. They are:

January 1	*Año Nuevo* (New Year's Day)
Friday before Easter	*Viernes Santo* (Good Friday)
May 1	*Día del Trabajador* (Labor Day)
May 25	*Revolución de Mayo* (Revolution of 1810 Day)
June 10	*Día de las Malvinas* (Malvinas Day)
June 20	*Día de la Bandera* (Flag Day)
July 9	*Día de la Independencía* (Independence Day)
August 17	*Día de San Martín* (Anniversary of San Martín's Death)
October 12	*Día de la Raza* (Columbus Day)
December 25	*Navidad* (Christmas)

and buses or drop them from high windows onto the street below. So much ticker tape falls from buildings, it seems to be snowing!

Diego Maradona

Diego Maradona's rise from poverty to fame and fortune is the kind of rags-to-riches story often associated with South American soccer stars. Maradona was born in a poor district of Buenos Aires in 1960. In his early teens, soccer-club scouts noticed Maradona's remarkable talent, and he started a professional career playing for Boca Juniors.

Although Maradona was regularly the Argentine league's top scorer, he did not play in the 1978 World Cup, which was held in Argentina. In 1982, he went to play in Europe, where he was very successful. He crowned this achievement by leading Argentina's team to victory in the 1986 World Cup final over Germany. At the height of his career, Maradona's turbulent personal life and problems overtook his playing talent. In 1994, aged 34, he went back to international soccer to help the Argentine team's World Cup challenge. Unfit and overweight, Maradona took drugs to try to improve his performance and received his second suspension for taking drugs. Despite this scandal Maradona remains popular in Argentina.

More than Football

The Argentines love their sports. The rich variety of landscapes gives opportunities for all kinds of games and pursuits. Tennis, golf, polo, horse racing, automobile racing, boxing, skiing, scuba diving, swimming, fishing, and especially soccer are just some of the many sports Argentines enjoy.

Soccer—*fútbol*—is an obsession in Argentina. The national team has won the World Cup twice, in 1978 and 1986. Passions run highest in Buenos Aires, where the rivalry of two of the local teams—Boca Juniors and River Plate—is legendary. Buenos Aires has many other local teams, and the city contains many soccer stadia. Games regularly attract crowds of between 45,000 and 75,000 fans. After Evita, the most famous of all Argentines is probably the soccer star Diego Maradona (*see* box).

Polo is a fast, exciting team game played on horseback.

Horses play an important part in Argentine traditional life, and two equestrian sports are particularly Argentine: polo and *pato*. Polo, a game between two teams of four players on horseback, was introduced to Argentina by the English in the mid-19th century. The riders use mallets with long, flexible handles to hit a small ball through the goals at each end of a large field.

Each polo game lasts about an hour, divided into short periods of play with three-minute rest intervals in between. There are one or two referees who are also on horseback, and another outside the playing area in case of disagreement. Argentina is the world's leading polo nation. Many of the best players live in Argentina and the best polo ponies are raised there. It is an expensive sport and usually played only by wealthy people.

Pato, by contrast, is one of the few sports native to Argentina and was first played by farm workers, many of whom were Indians. Someone once described the

How to Say...

Argentines are very friendly and welcome foreign visitors to their country. They like to chat and exchange opinions on the affairs of the day. They may even invite you to *tomar un mate* (share a *mate*) with them! Many Argentines, particularly those in Buenos Aires, speak English, but, as in every country, people are pleased when a foreigner tries to speak a few words of their language—however falteringly. Below are a few Spanish words and phrases that may be useful should you ever visit Argentina. A rough pronunciation follows in parentheses.

Please *Por favór* (por fa-VORR)
Thank you *Gracias* (GRA-see-as)
Yes *Sí* (SEE)
No *No* (NO)
Hello *Hola* (O-la)
Good bye *Adiós* (a-dee-OS)
See you later *Hasta luego* (AST-a loo-AY-go)
Good morning *Buenos días* (boo-AY-nos DEE-as)
Good afternoon *Buenas tardes* (boo-AY-nas TARR-des)
Good night *Buenas noches* (boo-AY-nas NO-ches)
How are you? *¿Qué tal?* (KAY TAL)
Sorry *Lo siento* (LO see-EN-toe)
Excuse me *Con permiso* (con per-MEES-o)
I understand *Entiendo* (en-tee-EN-doe)
I don't understand *No entiendo* (NO en-tee-EN-doe)
Do you speak English? *¿Habla inglés?* (AB-la in-GLAYS)
You're welcome *De nada* (day NA-da)
What is your name? *¿Cómo se llama usted?* (COM-o say zha-ma oos-TED)
My name is... *Me llamo...* (may ZHA-mo)
Sir/Mr. *Señor* (say-NYOR)
Madam/Mrs. *Señora* (say-NYO-ra)
Miss *Señorita* (say-nyo-REE-ta)

Numbers:

One/a *Un/una/uno* (OON/OO-na/OO-no)
Two *Dos* (DOSS)
Three *Tres* (TRACE)
Four *Cuatro* (KWA-tro)
Five *Cinco* (SINK-o)
Six *Seis* (SAY-iss)
Seven *Siete* (see-AY-tay)
Eight *Ocho* (O-cho)
Nine *Nueve* (noo-EV-ay)
Ten *Diez* (dee-ESS)

Days of the week:

Monday *Lunes* (LOON-ace)
Tuesday *Martes* (MARR-tace)
Wednesday *Miércoles* (mee-ERR-co-lace)
Thursday *Jueves* (HWE-bace)
Friday *Viernes* (vee-AIR-nace)
Saturday *Sábado* (SA-ba-doe)
Sunday *Domingo* (doe-MIN-go)

game as "basketball on horseback." *Pato* is the Spanish word for "duck"—originally the game was played with a live duck in a basket. Today the game is played by two teams of four horsemen. The duck and basket have been replaced by a leather soccer ball with six handles. The aim of *pato* is to score goals by punching or throwing the ball. When the ball falls to the ground, the players must lean down and pick it up by one of the handles at full speed, which requires skillful riding.

Education

At 98.8 percent, Argentina's literacy rate is one of the highest in Latin America and reflects the excellence of the school system. Between the ages of six and 14, school is free and compulsory. While almost all children in the big cities attend school, attendance is lower in more remote rural areas.

Junior high and senior high schools follow a system of education based on that of France. All children study the same subjects at the same time throughout the country; children cannot choose their subjects. Public schools are non-religious as they are in the United States. There are private schools, but the majority of pupils attend the free public schools.

University degree courses take four years or more. Traditionally, universities are free and open to all. Once a student has chosen his or her special subject, he or she studies that and nothing else. Because university education is free, many students continue their education. This has led to a surplus of doctors and lawyers in Buenos Aires, as these people are often not interested in working in rural areas.

There are 23 private universities, but the 29 public universities are considered better than their private equivalents. In recent years, the government has drastically reduced funding to the public universities. Nevertheless, a large proportion of young people still attend some form of further education.

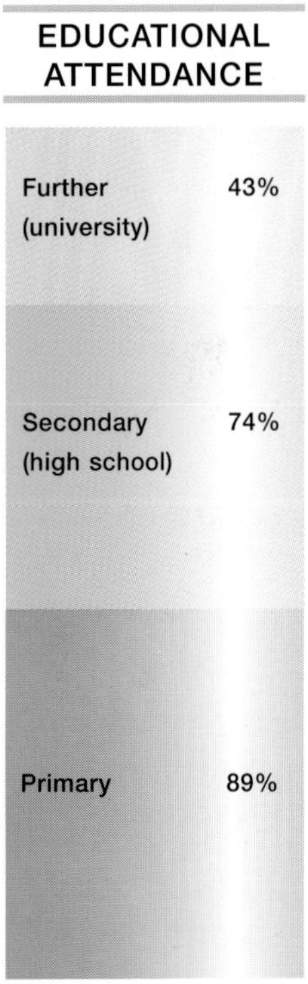

EDUCATIONAL ATTENDANCE

Level	Attendance
Further (university)	43%
Secondary (high school)	74%
Primary	89%

The Argentine education system is one of the best in South America. Further education remains strong, with students attending free national universities.

Argentine homes are generally not as well equipped as those of many Western nations, such as the United States.

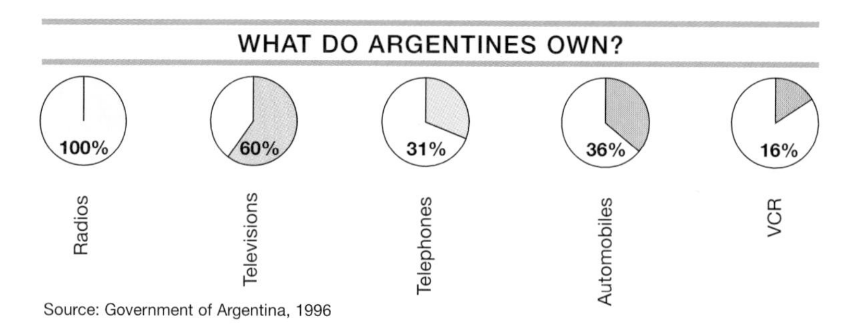

Health and Welfare

Argentina's medical system is one of the most advanced in Latin America. Hospital staff have often trained abroad as well as in Argentina. Specialists make a point of attending international medical conferences to keep up to date with worldwide developments.

Medical care is at its best in the major cities. In rural areas, the nearest doctor may be some distance away. There are some public hospitals that provide free emergency medical care, but generally the Argentine medical system is private. In 1992, there were some 376 people per doctor. The figure in Mexico was 1,000 people per doctor.

Life expectancy in Argentina is high. In 1998, it was calculated to be 69 years for men and 76 for women. Thanks to the modern health service, children have a good chance of survival and the infant mortality rate in 1997 was only 20 per 1,000 live births. Argentine families are small compared to the rest of Latin America. The average family has only two children, although rural families tend to be bigger. Argentina has more young people than older people: 30 percent of the population are aged 0–14, 57 percent are aged 15–59, and 13 percent are over 60.

The Argentine government spends about 2.5 percent of its gross national product (GNP) on health care.

Common causes of death are lung cancer—Argentines are heavy smokers—and road traffic accidents. Cases of HIV/AIDS (called SIDA in Spanish) have increased over the last few years. There are about 5,000 cases in Argentina, which is the second highest in South America, after Brazil, which has 55,000 cases.

The Argentine Media

Argentines love to follow the ups-and-downs of their favorite *telenovelas* (soap operas) on television. Most other programs are brought from the United States or Europe, but soap operas are produced locally, as are sports shows, game shows, and news programs. There are many more independent television channels than government-owned ones. There are some 12 government-owned and 30 independent television channels. With the legalization of non-state television and the arrival of cable TV, there is a greater choice of programming.

The most popular radio station is the nationwide Radio Rivadavia, which combines pop music and talk. In Buenos Aires alone, there are at least a dozen radio stations that specialize in different musical styles from classical and tango to rock music. There are some 75 private and 35 government-owned radio stations.

More than 200 daily newspapers are published in Argentina. Most are based in the provincial towns. The most important daily newspapers in Buenos Aires—*La Prensa, La Nación,* and *Clarín*—are also available nationwide. There are many weekly magazines that cover all aspects of life from the latest fashions to philosophical debate.

The *Buenos Aires Herald* is the only English-language newspaper in Argentina. It was founded in 1876 and is well known for being outspoken. During the military dictatorships, the newspaper wrote about human-rights abuses and condemned the people responsible.

The Future

"Dignity, justice, solidarity, and work."

Election slogan of Argentine president Fernando de la Rúa

At the beginning of the 20th century, Argentina seemed to have a glowing future. The country's situation was similar to that of two other newly independent nations, Canada and Australia. Its economy was booming, and the foundations of a modern democracy were in place. The country's abundant agricultural produce and the discovery of oil appeared ready to pay for the development of a modern industrial and transportation system. The capital, Buenos Aires, was a beautiful, lively city, whose cosmopolitan culture might easily one day rival that of the cities of Europe and America.

At the end of the century, however, much of the promise of a hundred years before had not materialized. Like many other countries, Argentina's democracy proved fragile. Military strongmen were able to exploit economic and social problems to set up regimes that abused human rights and weakened the economy. Domestically, Argentina remained underdeveloped, while internationally it found itself isolated and ignored.

Even the return to democracy in the early 1980s did not solve Argentina's problems or make up for wasted opportunities. At the end of the 1990s, inflation stood at a record low but unemployment was high. Hunger appeared in a country with plentiful food sources. For the first time, Argentina experienced some of the difficulties faced by its Latin American neighbors.

Many Argentine people look to the country's rich mineral resources as a way of revitalizing the ailing economy and building up new industries.

FACT FILE

- The dispute between Argentina and the United Kingdom over the Malvinas/Falklands looks likely to continue for some time. Both sides, however, have agreed to carry out joint oil exploration in the waters around the islands.
- Argentina promotes itself as a member of the "first world" of nations. For example, its army plays a role in the international peacekeeping missions of the United Nations.
- Argentina continues to develop economic ties with neighboring South American countries under the trading bloc MERCOSUR.

Argentina in Decline?

In the 1990s President Carlos Menem's harsh economic measures led to the government spending far less on such areas as education and health care. The negative effects of this policy are today being felt. Diseases such as cholera and tuberculosis have reappeared in a country that prided itself on having eliminated these diseases.

There is more unemployment and poverty, too, especially in the remoter parts of Argentina. More children are leaving school early because parents need them to start working to make a contribution to the family income. Lack of job prospects has also led to increased drinking and drug problems among the young.

Such difficulties have taken a heavy toll on the Argentines' pride. Many people—particularly *porteños* —saw their country as more European than Latin American. They have had to learn that perhaps, after all, they are not so different from their South American neighbors and that one solution to their country's problems lies in greater cooperation with countries such as Brazil, Bolivia, and Chile.

The Need to Diversify

Despite their difficulties, the Argentine people still have the potential to build a stable and prosperous nation. They have learned the hard lesson that they cannot rely on agricultural exports any longer and that they need to build up a wider variety of sources of national wealth.

One possible source of potential wealth is Argentina's rich mineral resources. Large oil, gas, and coal reserves were still largely

A New Direction?

In 1999, Fernando de la Rúa put an end to Carlos Menem's ten-year rule as Argentina's president. He won almost 50 percent of the vote in the presidential elections and brought to power a group of moderate (centrist) parties called the Alliance. While Menem was famous for his flamboyant personality, de la Rúa was thought of as an able administrator and hard worker. The new president wanted to build on Menem's economic reforms, cutting spending and increasing taxation, as well as continuing the program of privatization. In addition he aimed to introduce new welfare programs to help the poor, such as a food-voucher program.

untapped in the 1990s. President Carlos Menem encouraged private companies to search for new reserves. Increased energy output, it is hoped, will stimulate renewed interest in industrial growth.

Income from tourism is another potential growth area. Traditionally, tourism has been underdeveloped because of the long distances between Argentina and the United States and Europe. However, as air travel becomes cheaper, Argentina can potentially attract more visitors.

Argentina's membership in the Southern Cone trading bloc MERCOSUR proved important in the 1990s. However, some economists question whether MERCOSUR can last with only four member countries. They suggest that MERCOSUR might have to increase its trade by looking north to the North American Free Trade Association (NAFTA), which links the United States, Canada, and Mexico, or to the European Union (EU).

MERCOSUR

Members of MERCOSUR

Associate members of MERCOSUR

Non-members of MERCOSUR

The South American trading bloc MERCOSUR looks set to expand in the 21st century. Already two other Latin American countries—Chile and Bolivia—have become associate (part) members of the bloc.

Strengthening Democracy

After decades of destructive military rule, Argentina is determined to remain a democracy. President Menem reduced the military's power within Argentina, with the intention that it would never be able to take power again. The military now has a more international role and takes part in United Nations (UN) peacekeeping efforts.

On the other hand, many Argentine people believe that Menem too often flouted democratic institutions such as Congress, and that under his rule, corruption flourished throughout Argentine society. Many hope that President de la Rúa will be able both to keep the economy under control and strengthen the country's democracy.

Almanac

POLITICAL

Country name:
Official form: Argentine Republic
Local official form: *República Argentina*
Short form: Argentina

Nationality:
noun and adjective: Argentine or Argentinian

Official language: Spanish

Capital city: Buenos Aires

Type of government: federal republic

Suffrage (voting rights): everyone 18 years and over

Independence: July 9, 1816

National anthem: "*Himno Nacional Argentino*"

National holiday: May 25 (Revolution Day)

Flag:

GEOGRAPHICAL

Location: Southern South America; latitudes 22° to 56° south and longitudes 66° to 74° west

Climate: Arid in southeast; subantarctic in southwest, otherwise temperate

Total area: 1,072,156 square miles (2,776,884 sq. km)
land: 98.9%
water: 1.1%

Coastline: 3,100 miles (4,989 km)

Terrain: Plains in northern half; flat to rolling in south; rugged along western border.

Highest point: Aconcagua 22,843 feet (6,960 m)
Lowest point: Salinas Chicas -131 feet (-40 m)

Land use (1993 est.):
forests and woodland: 19%
arable land: 9%
permanent pastures: 52%
permanent crops: 1%
other: 19%

Natural resources: fertile plains, lead, tin, gold, copper, iron ore, oil, gas, uranium

Natural hazards: earthquakes, windstorms, flooding

POPULATION

Population (1999 est.): 36,737,664

Population growth rate (1998 est.): 1.4%

Birth rate (1999 est.): 19.91 births per 1,000 of the population

Death rate (1999 est.): 7.64 deaths per 1,000 of the population

Sex ratio (1999 est.): 97 males per 100 females

Infant mortality rate (1997 est.): 20 deaths per 1,000 live births

Life expectancy at birth:
- total population: 74.76 years (1999 est.).
- male: 69 years (1998 est.)
- female: 76 years (1998 est.)

Literacy:
- total population: 98.8%
- male: 98.8%
- female: 98.8%

ECONOMY

Currency: nuevo peso (P); 1 peso = 100 centavos

Exchange rate (1998): $1 = 1 P

Gross national product (GNP) (1996): $295 billion

Gross national product by sectors:
- agriculture: 7%
- industry: 37%
- service: 56%

Average annual growth rate (1990–1997): 5.4%

GNP per capita (1998 est.): $10,300

Average annual inflation rate (1990–1998): 19.3%

Unemployment rate (1998): 12%

Exports (1996): $23.8 billion
Imports (1996): $22.2 billion

Foreign aid received: $222 million

Human Development Index
(an index scaled from 0 to 100 combining statistics indicating adult literacy, years of schooling, life expectancy, and income levels):

88.8 (U.S. 94.2)

TIME LINE—ARGENTINA

World History		Argentine History
	***c.* 30,000 B.C.**	
***c.* 40,000** Modern humans—*Homo sapiens sapiens*—emerge.		***c.* 28,000** First inhabitants of the Americas settle in the continent.
	***c.* 10,000 B.C.**	
***c.* 10,000** Invention of bow and arrow.		***c.* 6000** First people settle in southern tip of Argentina, Tierra del Fuego.
	***c.* A.D. 100**	
***c.* 100** The Aztecs found Teotihuacán in Mexico. **900** The Vikings land in North America. **1200** The Incas build the city of Cuzco in Peru.		**650–850** Tiahuanaco empire in Bolivia and Inca empire in Peru influence the northern peoples of Argentina.
	***c.* 1500**	
1492 Columbus arrives in America—Europe begins period of exploration and colonization.		**1516** The Spaniard Juan Díaz is the first European to set foot in Argentina.
1522 Spanish ships led by Magellan complete the first circumnavigation of the globe. **1519** Hernán Cortés lands in Mexico.		**1536** Buenos Aires is founded by Pedro de Mendoza. **1528** The Italian Sebastian Cabot establishes the first Spanish settlement in Argentina, Sancto Spiritus.
	***c.* 1550**	
1620 Pilgrims land in New England. **1619** Europeans import the first African slaves to Virginia.		**1560–1700** Spanish colonists move through the country, building European-style cities, including San Luis, Tucumán, Mendoza, and Córdoba. **1608** Jesuits begin to set up missions in South America.
	***c.* 1700**	
1700 The Bourbon dynasty of kings begins its rule over Spain. The Bourbons reorganize Spain's colonies in South America.		**1767** The Jesuits are expelled from South America. **1776** Spain creates a new South American viceroyalty, Río de La Plata. The status and population of Buenos Aires increase.

c. **1800**

***c.* 1800** Spain is in decline as a world power.

1804 Napoleon crowns himself emperor of France.

1815 Napoleon is defeated at Waterloo.

1821 Mexico wins independence.

1859 British naturalist Charles Darwin publishes *Origin of Species.*

1861–1865 American Civil War

1810 The people of Buenos Aires form an independent government following a revolt.

1816 Argentina declares its independence at Tucumán on July 9.

1831–1836 Charles Darwin explores South America.

1835–1852 Juan Manuel de Rosas rules as a virtual dictator.

1853 Argentina adopts a federal Constitution on May 1.

c. **1900**

1914–1918 World War I

1929 The Great Depression begins.

1939–1945 World War II

1930 A military coup seizes power from the government.

1946 Juan Perón is elected president and sets about ruthlessly reforming Argentine society.

c. **1950**

1965 Start of U.S. involvement in Vietnam War.

1930 A military coup overthrows the elected government in Brazil.

1955 A military coup ends Perón's dictatorship; he flees the country.

1952 Eva Perón ("Evita") dies.

c. **1970**

1993 Bill Clinton becomes U.S. president.

1989 Democratic elections held in Chile.

1985 Civilian rule returns to Brazil.

1975 The Vietnam War ends.

1973 A military coup in Chile overthrows elected president, Salvador Allende.

1983 Democracy is restored to Argentina.

1982 South Atlantic War fought with Britain.

1976 Another military coup seizes power. The "Dirty War" against guerrilla groups begins.

1974 Perón dies.

1973 Perón returns to Argentina and is re-elected president.

c. **1995**

2000 The West celebrates the Millennium—2,000 years since the birth of Christ.

1999 Fernando de la Rúa becomes president.

Glossary

Abbreviation:
Sp. = Spanish

***audiencias* (Sp.):** Administrative bodies that ran realms within the Spanish viceroyalties of South America.

***barrio* (Sp.):** District in a city; especially Buenos Aires.

***caudillo* (Sp.):** Local leader who gained considerable power after Argentine independence.
colony: An overseas territory settled by another country.
conservative: Term used to describe political thought that places value on tradition and stability.
constitution: The fundamental principles that underlie the government of a country.
coup: The overthrow of a ruling power; often involving the use of violence.
***criollo* (Sp.):** Historically, someone of Spanish blood born outside Spain; creole.

democracy*:* A process that allows the people of a country to govern themselves, usually by voting for a leader or leaders.
dictator: A ruler who holds undemocratic power.

***encomienda* (Sp.):** The colonial system by which Spanish settlers were given land and Indian workers to work the land.

***estancia* (Sp.):** Large cattle ranch in Argentina.
exports: Goods sold by one country to another.
evolutionary theory: The idea that all species have developed from earlier forms.

gaucho: Argentine cowboy, who traditionally looked after herds of cattle on the Pampas.
glacier: Large, permanent mass of ice that forms over thousands of years.
gross national product (GNP): Total value of goods and services produced by the people of a country during a period, usually a year.
guerrillas: Non-government fighters with political aims; avoiding direct conflict, they use sabotage, raids, or ambushes as part of their campaign.

hydroelectricity: Electricity produced by harnessing the power released by falling or flowing water.

immigration: The arrival and settlement in a country of people from overseas. These people are known as immigrants.
imports: Goods bought by one country from another.
independence: The freedom of a nation or people from the rule of another nation.
inflation: The annual rate at which prices increase.

investment: The lending of money to businesses and organizations to allow growth and expansion.

Jesuits: Roman Catholic missionaries who follow the teachings of Ignatius of Loyola (1491–1556). In the colonial period, they set up missions in Argentina as well as in other South American countries.

landscape architecture: The creation of carefully designed gardens where land is developed for human use and enjoyment.
literacy: The ability to read and write.

***mestizo* (Sp. "mixed"):** Someone who has both Spanish and Indian ancestry.
mineral resources: Minerals that can be harnessed to provide energy or raw materials for manufacture.

nomadic: Term used to describe a lifestyle that involves migration from place to place in search of food or shelter.

***pampas*:** Flat plains.
Pampas, the: Grassland area covering most of the center of Argentina.
Patagonia: Dry, dusty tableland area in the south of Argentina.

Peronism: An Argentine political ideology based on the ideas of Juan Perón (1895–1974), involving strong government and national ownership of industries.
***porteño* (Sp.):** An inhabitant of the city of Buenos Aires.
privatization: The transfer of ownership and control of a business or organization to private individuals or companies.
protectionism: A government policy that "protects" home-produced goods by imposing high import taxes on products produced overseas.

steppes: Dry areas receiving less rain than prairies but more than deserts. Steppes are often covered in grass.
subtropical: A climate zone that borders on the tropical (between the Tropics of Cancer and Capricorn); subtropical regions are generally hot with periods of rainfall.

tableland: A large area of flat, high land.
tango: Music and dance style that originated in working-class areas of 19th-century Buenos Aires.

viceroyalty: A large administrative division of the Spanish colonies in the Americas.

Bibliography

Major Sources Used for This Book

Insight Guides: Buenos Aires. London, U.K.: APA Publications, 1996.
Foster, W. D., and others. *Culture and Customs of Argentina*. Westport, CT: Greenwood Publishing Group, 1998.
Nurse, C. *Argentina Handbook*. Bath, U.K.: Footprint Books, 1998.
Scobie, J. R. *Argentina: A City and a Nation*. Oxford, U.K.: Oxford University Press.
Williamson, E. *The Penguin History of Latin America*. London, U.K.: Penguin Books, 1992.

General Further Reading

Clawson, E. *Activities and Investigations in Economics*. Reading, MA: Addison-Wesley, 1994.
The DK Geography of the World. New York: Dorling Kindersley, 1996.
The Kingfisher History Encyclopedia. New York: Kingfisher, 1999.
Student Atlas. New York: Dorling Kindersley, 1998.

Further Reading About Argentina

Davies, H., and N. Irving. *Beginner's Spanish Dictionary (Usborne Language Books)*. Tulsa, OK: EDC Publications, 1989.
Kent, D. *Buenos Aires*. Cities of the World. Danbury, CT: Children's Press, 1998.
Lennon, A., and S. Samuels. *Jorge Luis Borges*. Hispanics of Achievement. Broomall, PA: Chelsea House, 1992.
Parker, S. *Charles Darwin and Evolution*. Science Discoveries. Broomall, PA: Chelsea House, 1995.
Parsons, M. *The Falklands War*. Sutton Pocket Histories. Gloucestershire, U.K.: Sutton Publishing, 2000.
Romain, J. and L. Goodall, eds. *Maradona*. Champion Sport Biographies. Toronto, Ont: Warwick Publishing, 1999.

Some Websites About Argentina

home.tampabay.rr.com/latinoconnect/argentin.html
www.latinworld.com/sur/argentina

Index

Page numbers in *italics* refer to pictures or their captions.

Acknowledgments

Cover Photo Credits
NHPA: Kevin Schafer (condor in flight); **Corbis:** Hubert Stadler (gaucho riding horse during roundup); **Tony Stone:** Robert Frerck (Plaza de Mayo)

Photo Credits
AKG London: 50, 52, 54; **Art Archive:** National Museum of History Lima 61; **Bridgeman Art Library:** Private Collection 53, 62, 96; Royal College of Surgeons London, UK 64; **Corbis:** Yann Arthus-Bertrand 56, 85; Bettmann 69; Bettmann/Reuters 75; Pablo Corral Vega 41, 89, 93, 115; Abbie Enock: Travel Ink 35; Owen Franken 72, 103, 106; John Garrett 116; Lowell Georgia 82; Robert van der Hilst 104; Kit Houghton Photography 6; Wolfgang Kaehler 18; Steve Kaufman 17; Graham Neden: Ecoscene 33; Enzo and Paolo Ragazzini 108; Fulvio Roiter 12; Galen Rowell 86; Hubert Stadler 21, 24, 42, 79, 80; TempSport 110; Adam Woolfitt 28; **Sylvia Cordaiy Photo Library:** J. Worker 73, 98; **Empics Limited:** Tony Marshall 90; **Hutchison Library:** Nick Haslam 100; B. Moser 78; **South American Pictures:** Kimball Morrison 63; Tony Morrison 59, 76, 94; **Tony Stone Images:** 31; Chad Ehlers 34; Robert Frerck 39, 40; George Haling 75; Oldrich Karasek 26; Michael Midgley 30; Dave Saunders 71; Alan Smith 22; Philip and Karen Smith 48; Robin Smith 46; John Warden 14; Thomas Zimmermann 111; **North Wind Pictures:** 32, 68.